First Wheel in Town:

A Victorian Cycling Club Romance

By Sarah A. Chrisman

Author of *Victorian Secrets, This Victorian Life*

Tales of Chetzemoka series:

First Wheel in Town
Love Will Find A Wheel
A Rapping at the Door

Other books by Sarah A. Chrisman
Victorian Secrets
True Ladies and Proper Gentlemen
This Victorian Life

For Gabriel

Chapter I

In the summer of 1881 everyone in the town of Chetzemoka was twitching with curiosity. The mystery revolved around a large crate which came addressed to Dr. Elijah Brown just before he was called away to Silas Hayes' bedside.

Hayes was a chronic invalid whose vague symptoms defied medical explanation. If his own accounts of his sufferings were to be believed, his condition existed in some bizarre, uncharted territory halfway between consumption and dyspepsia. If Hayes had been a poorer —or even a more amiable— man, the doctor would have diagnosed hypochondriasis and made sure his patient had plenty of outdoor work in the fresh Pacific Northwest air. However, the rich can afford to be sick for pleasure, and as nearly as Dr. Brown could determine, paid members of the medical profession were the only human beings willing to endure cantankerous old Mr. Hayes' company for more than five minutes at a time. The last trained nurse who had come to stay with him had endured eight months of martyrdom before moving on to the county insane asylum. Her replacement wasn't due for another three weeks, and Dr. Brown had promised to fill in during the interim.

In the meantime, the crate sat in the post office attracting everyone's attention.

Of all the curious people discussing the package, none took a more intense interest in the case than Kitty Butler, the dressmaker. The crate's return address declared it to be from the Weed

Sewing Machine Company, and an item which was pure curiosity to the rest of the community was — for her— a matter of professional interest.

A great deal of speculation went around town about what a bachelor like the doctor could possibly want with a sewing machine. The older married women theorized that the handsome young doctor must have a sweetheart he'd been keeping quiet about. Between comments about what a thoughtful and sensible gift it was, they traded guesses about his prospective bride's identity, and when the wedding would be. The unmarried women conferred with each other and determined that if the young doctor did indeed have marriage in mind, it wasn't with any of them. They made a mutual pact to shun whatever out-of-town usurper was planning to swoop in and steal property the young women of Chetzemoka considered as rightly belonging to themselves — that is to say, the doctor.

Kitty Butler (who at age twenty-six was the town's youngest widow and had been for the past four years) didn't fit in with either of the other groups, and she felt they were all on the wrong track. She knew just one thing about that crate: whatever was in it, it wasn't a sewing machine. The box was far too large. When Kitty heard everyone else conjecturing about some exotic new design of sewing machine none of them had seen before, she just shook her head privately and wondered how everyone could be so silly as to suppose that everything which came from a sewing machine company *must* be a sewing machine. They might as well call a fox a hen, just because they'd seen it leaving the hen-house.

Not that Kitty had any better idea than anyone else about what the doctor's crate actually did hold. Part of her wondered if it might have anything to do with an unusual order she'd made for him a week before: a canvas roll to hold the contents of his medical bag, after the fashion of the rolls army doctors use. Any time her thoughts strayed down that path however, she told herself it was just a woman's vanity —wanting to connect everything with herself. Otherwise she had no reason to suppose the one item had anything at all with the other.

By the time Dr. Brown got away from Mr. Hayes and was able to claim his package, the matrons were updating their best dresses for the expected wedding. The young ladies were sharpening their mental claws for a cat fight, and Kitty was hurrying to finish her orders ahead of time so she could close her shop for a few hours.

Town gossip determined that the new nurse was arriving on a steamer from Seattle at four p.m. on a Thursday. Kitty reasoned that by the time the doctor met the new arrival, showed her out to Hayes' mansion and saw her settled in with the patient, the post office would most definitely be closed. Considering how long he'd already waited for his package though, it was a safe bet he'd be there bright and early the next day. Kitty delivered her Friday orders on Thursday afternoon, wrote a short letter to her sister, and went to bed early.

Friday morning Kitty spent extra time arranging her hair, primping the ribbons on her dress and pinning the veiling fabric high on her bonnet so that her face would show. Even with this extra care she still left home early enough to arrive at the post office five minutes before it opened. As she'd expected, Dr. Brown was already there, waiting on the steps. There was a big grin on his face that reminded Kitty more of a schoolboy than of a grown man nearing his third decade.

*What **is** in that package?* She wondered as he tipped his hat to her and wished her good morning.

"Good morning," she returned his greeting. "Is that roll I made for you more convenient than your leather bag?"

His grin, if anything, grew broader. "Oh, it will be. Especially when I start doing rounds on my new machine!"

Before Kitty could ask what the doctor could possibly mean, the postmistress unlocked the doors and pushed one of them open. Dr. Brown caught it before it could swing shut again, and indicated that Kitty should precede him. She went inside then stopped short of the post office window, fingering her letter. "You were here before me," she told the doctor sweetly.

He nodded his thanks and strode up to the counter. One of the post office laborers was already dragging the crate out from the back. He handed Dr. Brown a pry-bar from the back pocket of his overalls and asked if he wanted a hand.

Dr. Brown declined the offer, and fell to prying open the crate with a vigor.

Kitty very carefully stayed out of the postmistress' line of sight and bit her lip with curious excitement as she watched the proceedings.

The inevitable excelsior was all that was visible when the first few slats came off the crate. After Dr. Brown had removed enough of the boards for the padding to start falling out of the wooden box, something curvy and nickel-plated was becoming visible through the straw-like wooden curls of excelsior.

*What **is** it?* Kitty sensed that she was seeing enough of the crate's contents to identify the "new machine" the doctor had mentioned, but she felt no closer to solving the mystery.

As more excelsior fell away, a wheel emerged. It was a very large wheel, nearly as tall as the doctor's shoulders.

Is it a spinning wheel of some sort? Kitty dismissed the ridiculous idea as soon as it occurred to her. In this modern age of steam mills which turned out thousands of yards of cloth in day, spinning was an eccentrically old fashioned hobby, even for a woman —let alone a modern-minded man like the doctor. She cast the idea aside and kept puzzling the matter.

Looking in more detail, she saw that the big, nickel-plated wheel had India-rubber around its rim, and what looked like sewing machine treadles sticking out of its center. There were two wooden handles sticking out of the top, and as the doctor brought the machine fully out of the box, Kitty finally saw that there was a much smaller wheel attached to it. Up near the handles was a leather pad of some sort whose function she couldn't even begin to guess.

She could see the whole machine at last, but Kitty was as much in the dark as she'd ever been.

The doctor leaned the wheel against the wall and stepped back to admire it. "Have you ever seen such a beautiful machine?" He asked very quietly, as if to himself.

He looked around for someone to share his reverie, and the first form his eye fell on was the laborer who'd loaned him the crowbar.

"Isn't she a beauty?" The doctor asked enthusiastically.

The laborer scratched the back of his head and stared at the doctor. "What do ye call that there thing?"

The broad grin the doctor had been wearing all morning shrank visibly. "It's a bicycle. I saw them for the first time in Boston—"

"And what's it fer?" The laborer interrupted, still scratching himself.

The smile shrank a little more. "Why, to ride, of course! Last year in Boston—"

The laborer guffawed. "Ter ride! 'Ter ride,' he says! Like he can't tell the difference 'atween a spinnin' wheel and a horse!"

Kitty was suddenly very ashamed that she had ever even thought to equate the pretty, nickel-plated creation in front of her with a spinning wheel. However the machine worked (and she was sure it *did* work, whatever the laborer said), it was lovely to look on.

"—Or maybe yer an old witchy-hag, like outt'en a fairy story, an' yer gonna ride yer spinnin' wheel cuz ya can't find yer broom?" The laborer slapped his thighs, laughing open-mouthedly and showing half-rotten teeth.

The doctor's smile was all gone now, and his customary dignity restored itself. "Thank you for letting me use this," he said coolly, handing back the pry-bar.

"MacGillivery!" Drawn by the bellowing, uncouth laughter, the postmistress looked sharply at the laborer. "Don't you think it's time you were getting back to work?"

MacGillivery retired to the back room, still slapping his thighs.

A shadow of the doctor's former smile returned to his face as he looked towards the postmistress. "Have you ever—" he began, but stopped short when he saw the way she pursed her lips at his wheel.

"We all thought it would be a sewing machine," she said with an air of bored disappointment. She returned to her place behind the counter and proceeded to sort the mail.

While everyone else's attention was diverted elsewhere, Kitty tucked her letter into her chatelaine purse, resolving to mail it later from home using one of the stamps she already had in her desk.

The doctor's sad look as he swept up the excelsior went straight to Kitty's heart. She tried several times to swallow the lump in her throat, and finally managed it when she saw Dr. Brown pat one of the wheel's handles, the way he might have patted a dog who'd been kicked.

"I think it's lovely!" Kitty called out meekly as Dr. Brown started pushing his wheel outside. She felt herself coloring as the doctor turned towards her, seeming to remember her presence there for the first time since he had unpacked the wheel.

He gave her a gentle smile. "Thank you."

Kitty suddenly wondered if it might be worth some sort of grave illness to wake up to the doctor's kind brown eyes every morning.

She turned towards the door and indicated that they should walk together. "What was it you were saying about Boston?"

Dr. Brown gave a wry grin, laughing at himself. "I went out there for my cousin's wedding last year." He took hold of the wooden handles atop the wheel and pushed it as he walked beside Kitty.

She was amazed at how smoothly it glided along. A thin line in the rubber had caught her attention when the wheel was stationary; tracking the wheel's motion by this line, she noticed that every time the wheel completed a revolution, the treadles in the middle likewise went around once in a circle. Seeing this tapped the same mechanical part of her brain that dealt with her sewing machine, but the analysis was a distraction from the Boston story. Since she had been the one who prompted the doctor to tell that story, she tried to pay attention to it.

"Her new husband—" the doctor continued the story about his cousin's wedding, "—is a member of the Boston Wheelmen, so the whole club turned out to salute the bridegroom."

A puzzled frown creased Kitty's brow. Dr. Brown, noticing the action, explained: "Boston has a social club for bicyclists, like an equestrian or a shooting club." He held his head a little higher and added, "Members are made up of some of the finest men in the city!"

Kitty nodded, showing she understood.

They reached the post office door and Dr. Brown performed the slightly awkward maneuver of opening the door for Kitty with his left hand while supporting his wheel with his right. She passed through and moved off to the side, then held her hand against the open door to keep it ajar while the doctor passed out with his wheel.

"Thank you."

His shoulder happened to brush against Kitty's hand as he came through the door, and she had to fight an urge to lean in closer, the way a cat would.

As she lifted the hem of her skirt to go down the post office steps, she wondered how Dr. Brown would manage the descent with his wheel.

To her surprise, the wheel descended the steps with remarkable grace, bumping only slightly as it went down each stair. Dr. Brown grinned at Kitty as he reached the bottom, wondering which direction she was going.

She inclined her head towards the least-traveled path in that part of the city.

Brown fell into step beside her, continuing his story. "The whole bicycling club showed up at the wedding in their uniforms—"

"Oh! What sort of uniform?" Kitty regretted the question as soon as she'd blurted it out. It was exactly the sort of silly, female query that annoyed men and convinced them of a woman's inanity. She tried comforting herself with the knowledge that at least she had a professional excuse for an interest in clothing. She'd never made a uniform, of course, but every woman with a uniformed beau or husband wanted him to complement her at dances, so Kitty sewed dresses to coordinate with uniforms all the time.

Unlike most men, Dr. Brown didn't drop a beat in the conversation when interrogated about a point of dress. He responded to Kitty's question with the same vim and vigor that had animated his every comment related to the bicycle since he'd unpacked it.

"The Boston club wears olive green, but they told me later that different clubs wear different colors. The jackets and caps aren't all that different from an army uniform. There's lots of frogging on the jackets." He paused in his description and a mischievous grin paired itself with a twinkle in his eyes. Like so much else about his attitude with the bicycle, it reminded Kitty of a schoolboy. "You'll never guess the bottom half of the uniform."

Kitty stepped around a hole in the path. "Well, if the jackets are patterned after military designs then I suppose the trousers—"

Dr. Brown chuckled softly.

Kitty blushed. She didn't think she'd said anything amusing, but nonetheless she ceased talking for fear of embarrassing herself.

"Not trousers." Dr. Brown said, shaking his head. "Can you believe it: they were wearing *knickers.*"

"*Knickers*!" Kitty stared at the doctor's face, wondering if he were teasing her. "Actual *short-pants*? But I thought these were grown men — some of the most eminent citizens in Boston, you said!"

Dr. Brown grinned and nodded. "That's exactly right —and they wear knickers for bicycling."

Kitty started walking again, shaking her head. "I can't believe it!"

"You have my oath on it, as both a doctor and a gentleman!" Brown assured her. He took up his place walking beside her again, still pushing his wheel.

"Knickers!" Kitty repeated, unable to overcome her astonishment. She shook her head, looking at the doctor. "If you had any idea how many knickers I've sewn, and every little boy begging his mother to put him in long-pants!" She imitated a chirping falsetto. "*Please, Ma, I'm ready for trousers! Please, Mrs. Butler, ma'am, ain't I old enough for long-pants?*" She returned to her normal voice. "Now you're telling me about a whole club of grown men who went back into short-pants willingly?"

Dr. Brown smiled. "I suppose they don't mind bicycling making boys of them all."

Kitty thought of how many times he herself had likened the doctor to a boy in the last hour since she'd greeted him on the post office where he waited to claim his wheel. Any shadow of doubt vanished, and she believed unreservedly in everything he was telling her. She started contemplating an entire group of men —powerful men, the best men in a large city like Boston— going about the city with their calves showing. And not just showing, but on display at the exact level a coquette's seemingly demure glance could best appreciate them. She looked down at the doctor's legs, and then straight into his mahogany-colored eyes. "I would like to see that."

The doctor's eyes grew wide at the bold gaze Kitty had turned on him. He swallowed visibly, as if just now remembering he was talking to a young widow and not a shy maiden. He tried to regain his composure as he walked on, but his wheel jogged his knee and caused him to half-trip, marring the effect.

There was a tree root in the path before them. Kitty lifted her skirt higher than she really needed, deliberately letting a flash of her silk petticoat peep out. She balanced atop the root for a moment, throwing a sly smile back at the doctor, then hopped down, skirts rustling.

Dr. Brown tried to follow with composure but his wheel bumped hard against the root, spoiling his attempt at dignity.

A few steps ahead of him, Kitty called back, "You never finished your story about Boston!"

"Oh!" Dr. Brown swallowed hard and cleared his throat. "The whole club showed up at church on their wheels—"

"In knickers!" Kitty inserted, with a mischievous glance downwards.

"In knickers," the doctor affirmed. "They were riding with their arms linked together in a formation bicyclists call a brace, and they were all singing "For He's A Jolly Good Fellow!""

Kitty smiled at the picture thus presented. "They must have scandalized the minister!"

Brown chuckled. "Oh, I don't think he minded much. I heard later that he'd been thinking of buying a bicycle himself. My aunt, on the other hand, was positively livid! I've never seen a bride's mother turn so many shades of red so quickly!"

Kitty laughed, a sound like the chiming of bells.

Brown looked suddenly sheepish, as if aware he was coming to a part of the story she might think reflected unfavorably on him. He forged ahead, all the same. "She still hasn't forgiven me for staying outside chatting with the lad who'd been left to guard the wheels so long I missed the whole wedding ceremony."

Kitty's jaw dropped in shock. "Oh, Dr. Brown, really? After you'd taken the train all the way across the country to be there for it? If I were your cousin and you'd snubbed my wedding that way, I'm not sure I'd forgive you very quickly either!"

"Oh, no —my cousin didn't mind! I confessed to her at the dinner afterwards. She just chucked me under the chin and said I was just like her new husband, and that he was bringing his wheel on their honeymoon with them. It's my aunt who's still in a stew over it!"

Kitty chuckled. "Well, if the bride forgave you, she's the one who matters!"

She climbed atop another tree root, doing the same trick where she let her petticoat peep forth just a bit. She discretely slid her fingers and wrist in such a way as to make the silk rustle as loudly as possible without showing any signs that she was overtly causing the sound at all. It was a trick any woman with a silk petticoat knows, but a dressmaker does best. She gazed back at the doctor, and she saw how clearly he had heard the sound of the silk.

He hurried after her and she let out a laugh. She turned away quickly and hopped from the root without looking down.

In midair she glanced downwards and an abrupt scream escaped her. A huge, black and yellow snake lay right on the path beneath her.

Terrified, Kitty tried to stop her motion, to go back. But she'd put too much momentum into her step when she'd sprung forward without looking.

She came down on top of the snake and felt a terrifying, thrashing slithering amid her skirts.

She screamed again, turning and leaping over the root.

Dr. Brown had dropped his wheel and rushed forward at Kitty's first shriek. He saw a streak of black and yellow disappear into the brush just as Kitty collided with him.

She tried to go past him and keep running, but he caught her and spoke in a reassuring, gentle tone. "Shh... Shh! It's alright! You're okay! It was just a garter snake. A big one, and in a bad place, but just a garter snake."

Kitty fell against Dr. Brown's chest, hiding her face in his shoulder while her whole frame trembled. He kept saying calm, reassuring things to her until she stopped shaking, but even then she kept her face buried in his shoulder for long moments.

When he felt wetness there, vague memories floated to his mind's surface, tales told in passing by people for whom they were old news. He'd come to Chetzemoka after Kitty had left off mourning, but small towns tell everyone's tragedies.

Kitty moved away at last, and fumbled in her purse for a handkerchief. "You must think me terribly silly, to get so scared and then fall apart over a snake." She spoke shamefully, wiping her eyes.

"No, no! It's alright." The doctor considered avoiding the painful subject, but this seemed like a case where a wound needed lancing to heal. "It was a snake, wasn't it, that spooked your husband's horse? That's how he broke his neck?"

Kitty nodded sadly, wiping her eyes, then her nose. "Not even married a year, and I had to dye my bridal gown and turn it into widow's weeds. A part of me almost wanted to shoot that horse, I was so angry."

She took a full, bracing breath. "But, instead I sold it to someone leaving town, so I'd never have to see it again. And I used the money to get started in my dress shop." She pressed her lips together and nodded briskly, once, as if casting off things that were done and over. "But I'll always hate snakes." She concluded firmly. "I will always hate snakes!"

Dr. Brown nodded understandingly. "Would you like me to walk you back to your rooms —or to your shop?"

Kitty sighed, wiping hands over her red cheeks to cool them. She glanced in the direction of the path to her lodgings, then gave the doctor a sad smile. "No, it's alright. Thank you, but—" She looked at the trees around them. "I'd just like to be alone for a while."

Dr. Brown nodded again. "If there's anything I can do for you, anything at all, please just ask."

Kitty smiled her thanks, and nodded. She unpinned the veil on her bonnet and lowered it to hide her face, then started to walk away.

She was stopped by the doctor's wheel, which lay across the path where he had dropped it. "Doctor?" She turned back towards him.

"Yes, ma'am?"

"This wheel of yours, it's really for riding, like a horse?"

"That's right."

She looked down at it for a long moment. When she spoke again it was to ask a question very softly. "But a machine would never spook like a horse, would it?"

"No ma'am." He assured her confidently, lifting up the wheel. "No ma'am, it would not."

It was hard to judge subtle expressions through the veil, but he thought he read approval between the lines of crisscrossed silk.

Kitty nodded, and slowly parted from him.

Chapter II

The doctor very much regretted the incident with the snake. As excited as he was about his new bicycle, he'd have thrown it in Puget Sound before willingly causing Kitty Butler grief. The whole occurrence had been completely unpredictable though, and one of the hard lessons his medical practice had taught him was that unpredictable is synonymous with unavoidable.

As he continued along the path out of town, he felt somewhat ashamed to admit that —for him at least— the mishap had a bright side. He hadn't wanted Kitty to see him making a fool of himself while he practiced riding his new bicycle.

Brown had caught "wheel fever" from his first sight of the Wheelmen riding in Boston. If his savings hadn't been completely denuded by his trip across the country and an expensive tea service he'd bought his cousin as a wedding present, he'd have gleefully run to the nearest bicycle agent and bought one for himself right away. As things stood, however, he'd had to be content with borrowing one.

It hadn't been easy. The bicyclists were profoundly unwilling to lend out their machines. When Brown mentioned it, the expression on each man's face reminded him of a parrot in a popular joke: though he said little, he thought a great deal.

At last, one of them took Brown aside and confided: "You've heard the saying that a gentleman never lends out 'a pipe, a pen, or his wife'? Well, most of us Wheelman are as attached

to our machines as we ever were to a woman."
The Wheelman's eyes gained a soft, far-away look.
"You ride a machine every spare moment, every
sunny day (and even the rainy ones), and well, it
just becomes a part of you. You don't want to see
it in another man's hands any more than you'd
want to watch another man taking your
sweetheart to a dance —no matter how good of a
sort he is. And when someone who's never ridden
a bicycle before asks to borrow one, the man he
asks remembers back on every tumble and scrape
he took while learning to ride. Now, ask yourself
honestly sir: Would you really feel comfortable
watching your sweetheart marched off to a dance
by a man you knew was going to step all over her
dainty feet, and maybe ruin her pretty shoes? No
matter how good of a fellow he was, I contend sir
that you'd be other than human to not have a
single misgiving about it."

After that speech, Brown was afraid he'd
never ride a wheel until he'd replenished his
savings enough to afford one of his own.

The next day he'd seen one of the
Wheelmen teaching his young son to ride, and had
sat down to watch them. The bicyclist's wife and
daughter sat nearby, occupying themselves with a
very large picnic hamper and a very small poodle.
When the dog started choking on a chicken bone
and Brown sprang to the rescue, both the girl and
her mother were so grateful that they insisted
Brown's wish for riding lessons be granted.

As Dr. Brown's ill luck would have it, the
man whose dog he'd rescued happened to be the

very tallest member of the Boston Wheelmen. His club nickname was Jumbo, after the London Zoo elephant P.T. Barnum kept trying to buy. Even though Brown himself was of average height, when he stood next to Jumbo he felt like they were pantomiming one of the cartes-de-visites from Barnum's old American Museum, where giants were set up next to dwarves for contrast. When Jumbo nervously explained that bicycles are sized to leg length like trousers, Brown nearly despaired. However, Mrs. Jumbo was very insistent that her husband should show sufficient gratitude for Brown having saved their dog; and so Brown learned to ride on Jumbo's bicycle —which was of course, far too big for him.

The first time Brown tried to mount the 58-inch wheel, both man and bicycle keeled over sideways. On his second attempt he did manage to leap into the saddle, but split his trousers in the process. When he tried to dismount, the torn fabric caught on the seat of the bicycle and Brown found himself doing a very rapid circumnavigation of the wheel. He landed flat on his back in a bed of freshly manured petunias. The very wheel he had been riding ran *him* over; and Jumbo's son (who was watching nearby) nearly busted a gut laughing.

It had been exactly the sort of scene Brown did not want Kitty Butler to see on the day his own wheel arrived.

Finding a vacant stretch of road outside Chetzemoka, Brown reminded himself of everything Jumbo had taught him while he'd been in Boston.

"Wheels in line," he told himself, carefully aligning the small stabilizing wheel behind the large driving wheel that powered the machine.

"Get it going—" He pushed the bicycle, running beside it.

"Foot on the step—" He caught the small step on the bicycle's backbone with his left foot.

"—And swing over!" His right leg swung over the saddle, his foot caught the pedal, and as the motion caused the pedal on the other side to swing up, his left foot caught that one.

He was riding!

Brown was amazed at how much easier it was on this wheel than it had been on Jumbo's. He remembered the tall man's comment about a bicycle being sized to leg length, "like a pair of trousers." On Jumbo's wheel Brown had barely been able to reach the pedals; on this —his own bicycle, his own size— every stretch of his legs skimmed him over the road with ease and amazing speed.

Brown had gained considerable self-assurance by the time he stopped. Unfortunately, his dismount put a dent in that confidence.

Before setting out to claim his wheel at the post office that morning, Brown had dressed in the roughest clothes he owned —a coarse flannel shirt and an ancient pair of trousers he wore when he chopped wood. He'd felt awkward encountering Kitty Butler that way, but it couldn't be helped. His usual suits were too stiff and restrictive for sport, and he didn't want to tear the seat out of another pair of trousers.

Unfortunately, that's exactly what he did as he swung his leg around to get off his wheel.

At least this time he landed on his feet, and there was no one else around to fill his burning ears with laughter. Inspecting the damage, Brown considered that perhaps his most threadbare trousers hadn't been the best choice for this activity.

He reached down and measured the rent with his hand. It reached as wide as his fingers could stretch —and then some. He shook his head, sorry that his practice run should end so abruptly, but very glad he had chosen such a lonely place for it.

A few minutes later he would wish it was even more deserted.

As Brown walked his wheel back towards the rented rooms where he lived, he thought of the knickers the Boston Wheelmen wore. Jumbo had loaned Brown a pair after he'd torn his trousers the first time, and he thought he might be due a pair of his own.

Even though tall Jumbo's knickers had fit Brown almost like long-pants, he remembered a remarkable feeling of freedom while wearing them. Something about the way they were cut made the fabric stretch in ways wool usually wouldn't; otherwise he didn't think he'd have ever managed to mount Jumbo's enormous wheel. Pondering how much easier it already was to ride his own (properly sized) bicycle, Brown took a great deal of pleasure from imagining how the right clothes would facilitate matters even more.

The sharp call of a flicker woodpecker broke into Brown's reflections. He looked ahead and saw two vibrantly colored flickers, one male, one female, following each other in a slow, elaborate dance around the trunk of a fir tree. The male (obvious from his feathery scarlet mustache), flashed the bright orange undersides of his tail feathers at the female and called to her, then took a few steps spiraling up the tree and peeped at his lady love from the other side of the trunk. She coyly followed, careful not to overtake him but always keeping him in sight. He flashed his bright tail, stepped away, peeped at her, and repeated the whole process, all the while puffing up his speckled breast.

On a mossy boulder near the flickers' tree, Kitty sat watching the birds.

Brown wondered if he could retreat without being noticed. Unfortunately, the sunlight flashed ostentatiously off of Brown's nickel-plated wheel, and caught Kitty's attention right away. She looked straight at him and smiled softly, pressing a finger to her lips. She pointed at her eyes, then at the birds and went back to watching them.

Brown assessed his choices. He guessed he was still too far away for Kitty to see the gaping hole in his trousers —from this direction. If he retreated the way he had come, it would be dreadfully obvious if she glanced his way at all.

Continuing down the path and approaching closer to her was out of the question.

Brown was still trying to work out a solution when the birds flew away together and Kitty stood up. She gave Brown another soft smile and started walking towards him.

Well, that's pitched it! Seeing few good options for himself, Brown quickly set his bicycle down in the road and stepped into the greenery at the side of the trail. He felt ridiculous, but at least now everything from his elbows down was obscured.

Kitty's smile was immediately replaced by utter astonishment. "Why, Dr. Brown, whatever are you doing?"

"Oh, nothing! Nothing!" He tried to sound casual. "I just thought I saw a flower for you here in the—" He stopped as he realized what sort of greenery he'd run into. "Stinging nettles," he finished weakly. He hadn't thought he could possibly be *more* aware of the enormous hole in his trousers than he had been when he'd seen Kitty in front of him. Suddenly though, this was very much the case.

"Oh, for goodness sakes!" Kitty's jaw dropped. "Don't be absurd. Get out of there right this minute!"

Brown swallowed, hard. "Yes, of course. I don't know what I was thinking. But —I'm sorry, Mrs. Butler— would you mind turning around, please? And do you happen to have such a thing as a housewife about you?"

Kitty looked puzzled for just a second, then understanding dawned over her face. She seemed to smother a giggle and her eyes flitted downwards for the briefest instant, then she obligingly turned her back on Brown. She reached into her purse. "Of course I have a housewife, Dr. Brown. I am a dressmaker, after all!" She took it out, then held it behind her back where Brown could reach it.

He breathed a deep sigh of relief as he took the small embroidered packet holding needles and thread. He had been sincerely worried about what he was going to do when he reached the populated section of town. He lived in one of the busiest parts of Chetzemoka, and it wouldn't do his practice any good at all if half the town saw their doctor wandering around with split trousers. "Thank you!"

"Oh, it's—" Kitty almost turned around automatically when Brown spoke to her, but she managed to stop herself. "—No trouble."

Changing the subject, she nodded towards the tree the birds had been spiraling. "Had you seen a woodpecker wedding before?"

Brown followed Kitty's gaze, surprised at the question. "Is that what they were doing?"

She nodded. "I came across them, and stopped to watch as they went from tree to tree. It was calming, and very —sweet."

Brown couldn't see Kitty's face, but he thought a smile crept into her voice.

"—And now they've flown off to their honeymoon!" She concluded. "And I should be going myself, so I can let you do that mending. Just bring the housewife back to me at my shop tomorrow. I'll be there from ten until three. You know where it is, don't you?"

"It's next door to the tailor's shop in the Hastings building, isn't it?"

"That's right," With her back still turned towards Brown, Kitty nodded, then started walking away. "I'll see you tomorrow!"

"Good-bye, Mrs. Butler!" Brown called after her.

Kitty diligently kept her back towards Brown until she reached a twist in the road, where the path curved to avoid a particularly large Douglas fir. Passing around the tree, she peeped back quickly around its trunk, and glimpsed the doctor once more before continuing on her way.

Chapter III

The next day Brown arrived at the Hastings building with Kitty's housewife in his pocket. Before going to her shop, he bounced through the door of Short's Tailor Shop next door and found Mr. Short pinning a frock coat which hung on a form. Behind him, an open window let a slight breeze —and the smell of low tide— into the hot room.

"Good morning!" Brown flashed the tailor an exuberant smile. "I'm here to order a bicycling suit!"

Mr. Short frowned at him through turn-pin spectacles. His clothes were of the very latest style, but Dr. Brown couldn't help noticing that his eyeglasses were of a design which had been outdated for decades. "I'm sorry, sir," Short said to the doctor. "I didn't quite hear you. What sort of a suit, did you say?"

"A bicycling suit!" Brown repeated cheerfully. He described the uniforms he had seen in Boston: quasi-military jackets, and knickers.

Mr. Short looked irritated and went back to pinning the coat. "I'm sorry, sir. I don't do costumes for fancy-dress parties. I have far too much real work to occupy me."

"Oh, no, no!" Brown stepped around the tailor's form to put himself back in the man's line of sight. "This wouldn't be for anything of the sort! It's for riding a wheel!"

"Riding a wheel?" The tailor repeated slowly. "I'm sure I don't know what you mean, sir."

"Bicycling!" Brown grinned. "If you've never seen a bicycle, I really must show you mine. I just unpacked it yesterday. A bicycle is the most beautiful machine you can imagine —simply a marvel of modern technology! Why, what would you say to a horse that takes up barely a few feet of space, never needs pasturing, and feeds off of only a few drops of oil?"

The tailor managed to look dubious and condescending at the same time, as though he were speaking to a harmless madman. "A mechanical horse?" He took off his spectacles and polished the conservative lenses through which he viewed the world. "If you're asking for a suit of play clothes to go with some sort of children's toy, you'll have to bring the boy in to be measured."

"No!" Brown shook his head. "That's not it at all! A bicycle isn't a toy. It's the latest in modern vehicles. It has two wheels, with pedals on the bigger one to turn it—"

The tailor smirked patronizingly as he replaced his eyeglass stays over his ears. "A velocipede? Sir, those went out more than a decade ago."

Almost as long ago as those spectacles of yours, Brown thought, growing irritated. He held his tongue though, as the tailor continued.

"Sir," the man went on. If someone has convinced you those old boneshakers are the latest thing, I am afraid you've been swindled."

"No!" Brown insisted. "A bicycle no more resembles a velocipede than a racing stallion does a plough horse. To start, the bicycle's tires are rubber, not iron, and instead of wooden wheels—"

"Sir, I really am quite busy!" The tailor broke in curtly. "I don't have time to hear about some odd contrivance to which you've taken a fancy. Would you please state your business here today?"

"I came to order a suit of clothes! Knickers, and a matching jacket. Cut to make them stretch —you'd know more about that than I would, I suppose."

The tailor looked down his nose at Brown, over his glasses. "Are you seriously proposing," he asked slowly, emphasizing each word. "—That I produce knickers for a grown man? *Knickers*, sir?"

Brown's cheerfulness was gone. Now he just wanted his order taken. "That's right. Cut so they'll stretch."

"Sir!" The tailor drew all his dignity together as he squared his shoulders and held his head high. "The very idea of *knickers* for a *grown man* is absurd! I would never dream of it. If you were to appear in public in such a costume, you'd be the laughing stock of the city for the rest of your days. Before you take such strange fancies into your head, you'd do well to consider what it would do to your practice. After all, you aren't the only doctor in Chetzemoka, and I don't know anyone who would trust their health and life to a man who goes prancing about in public dressed like a little boy. *I*, for one, will have no part in it. Good day, sir!" He turned his back on Dr. Brown.

Brown was flabbergasted at the speech.

He left the tailor's shop crestfallen, all his high hopes and dreams for the day beaten down. In retrospect, he considered that the reactions at the post office the previous day might have warned him of this sort of hostility, but he simply hadn't wanted to believe people could be so closed-minded.

He'd been yearning after a wheel of his own ever since he'd gone to Boston. The entire year past, he'd been dreaming of how proud he'd be to ride it on all his rounds, and in his spare time too. He'd imagined himself the envy of the town, inspiring every other man in Chetzemoka to buy bicycles of their own. He thought they might even start a club. He'd never dreamed that other people wouldn't see the beauty of the glorious machine. It was so obvious to him.

Brown paused in the hallway outside the tailoring shop and sighed. Short was the only tailor in Chetzemoka, and the towns out here on the Olympic Peninsula were so widely spaced that taking a steamer all the way down to Seattle would probably be easier than renting a horse to get to a smaller town. And a steamer trip to Seattle would take all day —at least. If he missed the steamer back to Chetzemoka he'd be stuck in Seattle overnight. He might even be stuck there two nights, since the steamer didn't run on Sundays. Things would have been frustrating enough if there had been an actual, legitimate reason Short

34

couldn't do the work. If he'd been backed up in orders, or was leaving on vacation, Brown would have understood. But this blank, pointless refusal to take a paying customer's money, simply for reasons of ignorant prejudice —well, it pained the heart.

Brown kept trying to think of a solution as he put a hand into the pocket in the tails of his frock coat, reaching for his gloves.

It would be easy to ride to another town on his wheel —if he had anything to wear while riding it. But since he couldn't ride the wheel until he had riding clothes, it was a real conundrum. He smiled wryly at the irony.

Next to the leather gloves in his pocket, Brown's fingers encountered a small, embroidered packet. He remembered the housewife, and drew it out. He ran his thumb over the embroidered cat on its cover, peeping out from Kitty's stylized initials, "K.B." Then he frowned at the door of her dress shop, next door to the tailor's.

After the encounter with Short, Brown really wasn't in any sort of mood to be sociable right then. He thrust the housewife back into his pocket, thinking there couldn't be any harm in waiting to return it. *After all,* he told himself, *it's not like a dressmaker doesn't have needles and thread to spare.*

He had just started to walk away when he heard a door open behind him.

"Dr. Brown?"

The sweet, feminine voice stopped him in his tracks. He turned back around, and as he met

Kitty's soft blue eyes, he was ashamed of himself for trying to slink away. He tipped his hat to her. "Good afternoon, Mrs. Butler."

"Good afternoon, Dr. Brown." She beckoned him into the shop and closed the door behind him. She paused then and gazed towards her window, something clearly on her mind.

Neither of them spoke for a long moment. Brown noticed that Kitty's window was shut, yet the room held a distinct scent of the sea outside.

"It's hot today," Kitty said at last.

Brown agreed.

"I had my window open—" she continued.

Brown remembered the open window in the tailor's shop next door, and suddenly realized Kitty's words were more than the usual pleasantries about the weather.

"Have you ever noticed how shrill Mr. Short's voice is, for a man?"

Brown started to smile, then caught himself and controlled his expression. "I suppose you're saying that you heard our conversation?" He asked.

Kitty nodded. "You know," she said, crossing to a tall cupboard. "Mr. Short really doesn't make many knickers, anyways." She swung the cupboard door open, revealing a tall stack of neatly folded boys' short-pants. "I do."

The shocked look on Dr. Brown's face made Kitty laugh. "You're such a bachelor, Dr. Brown." She told him. "Who made your knickers when you were a boy?"

"Well, I—" Brown stammered. "I hadn't thought of that for years." He considered the question. "I guess, when I think of it, it was my mother."

Kitty nodded. "It usually is. Unless the mothers are too taken up with other work or have no skill with a needle. When that's the case — well, quite frankly, I charge less than a tailor, and most women would usually rather deal with me, anyways."

After this short, simple speech, Brown looked from Kitty to the stack of knickers and back again, at a loss for words.

"Now!" Kitty rubbed her chin, giving him an appraising look. "I assume you'll want a lightweight wool for this?"

"Cut—" Brown began automatically.

"—On the bias, so it'll stretch. Of course." Kitty completed his statement for him absently, walking to a corner where bolts of fabric were lined up against the wall. She started flipping through them. "I have some nice cloth that was going to be an equestrian dress for Mrs. Snow, but she changed her mind." Kitty drew out a bolt of hunter-green tweed. "There now—" She unrolled a section of fabric and held it up next to Brown, evaluating. "The color's good with your dark hair and beard. I have enough here for two suits like you described —if you really are going to do your rounds on your wheel, you'll want a spare riding suit, for laundry purposes."

Kitty was being so matter-of-fact about things, Brown automatically followed her to a tall cheval glass which stood nearby. He nodded at his reflection, agreeing with her assessment. Then he stopped himself.

"Now, wait a minute!" He turned towards Kitty. "Let's just be clear: are you offering to make knickers for me?"

She met his gaze frankly. "Why not?"

Brown swallowed hard. He wondered what it would be like to have his measurements taken by a woman, by Kitty. Being measured by a man was one thing, but—

He thought of all that was so very feminine about Kitty: the clacking of sewing tools on the chatelaine at her waist, the rustle of her silk petticoat, the smell of lavender issuing from somewhere deep within the folds of her clothes. He glanced down involuntarily at his inseam, and was glad that his whiskers probably hid the fact that he was blushing like a girl.

Kitty smirked and took the measuring tape off her chatelaine. "Shall we get started?"

Chapter IV

Early the next morning Kitty stood before the door of Brown's lodgings, rubbing her eyes. She had a large package under one arm, wrapped in brown paper. At her knock, the doctor's landlady answered the door wiping her hands on an apron.

"Why, Mrs. Butler!" The ruddy-complexioned woman said with surprise. "Is everything alright? Are you here for the doctor?"

"Oh, yes, everything's fine, Mrs. Ostergren!" Kitty assured her. "I'm sorry, I suppose it is rather early to be calling. I'm just dropping this off for the doctor." As she took the package from under her arm, the man himself came up behind Mrs. Ostergren.

"Mrs. Butler!" Brown looked as surprised as his landlady.

Mrs. Ostergren looked back at her boarder, and something about his expression when he saw the younger woman made her smirk. Mrs. Ostergren straightened her apron and held the door open for Kitty. "Well, you might as well come in and have a cup of coffee."

Behind Mrs. Ostergren's back, Dr. Brown made a horrified expression and shook his head.

Seeing Kitty's attention drawn to Brown, the landlady looked back at her boarder. He immediately wiped away the disgusted look on his face and flashed Mrs. Ostergren a grin which struck Kitty as more than a little forced.

Kitty couldn't begin to guess what all this was about, but her eyelids were drooping and the idea of coffee was very welcome. She eagerly took Mrs. Ostergren up on her offer.

When the landlady turned to lead the way to the dining room, Brown mouthed something at Kitty. She thought it looked like, "I tried to warn you." She couldn't be sure, though.

Mr. Ostergren was seated at the head of the dining room table reading a copy of the local newspaper, *Chetzemoka Leader.* When his wife told him that Mrs. Butler had come in for coffee, he gave Kitty a look which mingled pity with apology in equal measures.

The remains of a dish of hash were on the table. The china ware was beautiful, dainty, and clearly expensive. The food, on the other hand, looked distinctly unappetizing. The Ostergren children gazed at it glumly. They looked hungry, yet indecisive.

Mrs. Ostergren disappeared into the kitchen. Brown pulled out a chair for Kitty, and sat down next to her. "Now," he asked. "What brings you here so early?"

Kitty held up her package. The Ostergren children perked up, as though wondering if it might contain something to eat. "I brought your knickers, and the jacket and cap that go with them." Kitty told Brown. "I can make the second suit we talked about by next week."

The children sunk down again with sulky, disappointed expressions. Mr. Ostergren let the top of his newspaper fall and gazed over it curiously.

Brown took the package and gazed at Kitty in a new light. "You didn't have to make it a rush order," he told her after a long pause.

She smiled shyly at him. "I knew it was important to you."

Just as Brown was thinking he could drown in the deep blue pools of Kitty's eyes, Mrs. Ostergren came out of the kitchen with the coffee pot and broke the spell.

As Mrs. Ostergren set a delicate china cup in front of Kitty, the oldest Ostergren boy spoke up. "Is there any more bread, Ma?"

The other children, seemingly emboldened by Kitty's presence, echoed the request. "Yes, bread!" "We'd like some bread, Ma!"

Mrs. Ostergren glanced at Kitty, blaming her for this insubordination. Then she gave her children a stern look. "Here, now! You know I don't like to cut any more than I think you'll eat. It goes stale so quickly. Eat the hash, if you're still hungry."

The children stared glumly at the hash again. It seemed to contain an unappetizing quantity of codfish balls mixed in with the meat, and judging from the burnt material around its edges was on its second or third reheating. The youngsters looked morosely back at their plates.

Mr. Ostergren saw a need to change the subject. "Mrs. Butler," he asked pleasantly, turning towards their unexpected guest. "What was that you were saying about knickers?"

Kitty and Dr. Brown exchanged conspiratorial grins.

Mrs. Ostergren poured something black into Kitty's cup. (It smelled more of fish and burnt chicory than of coffee.) The rubicund woman cast a curious look at the brown paper parcel Kitty had carried in. "Knickers?"

Kitty added as much cream as her cup could hold and sipped sparingly at the disgusting concoction. Meanwhile, Brown eagerly launched into the story of the Boston Wheelmen and their uniforms. After he had finished, the Ostergrens stared at him in silence a long moment.

"Grown men in knickers?" Mr. Ostergren asked at last. He had the good manners to try and keep his tone level. "Well, that's... interesting."

"You're saying—" Mrs. Ostergren broke in, in tones of dark disapproval. "—That this is all about that *thing* you brought in the other day?" Her brows were furrowed very low. "If you scrape up my wallpaper resting those handles against it, Sir, I'll charge you for it! Don't think I won't!"

Brown assured Mrs. Ostergren that he would be careful. Then another uncomfortable silence fell.

Kitty sipped at the liquid in her cup, trying hard to just pull the cream off the top without disturbing what lay beneath it. She wasn't entirely successful, and by the time she'd drawn off all the cream her stomach was beginning to curdle. She kept up a brave face though, and smiled over at Brown. "Do you think you'll be riding at all this morning?" She asked casually.

Mrs. Ostergren looked shocked. "What about church! You don't mean to say he should skip services?"

Brown consulted his watch, then grinned at Kitty. "There's still a little time. I think it's an excellent idea!"

Kitty excused herself and waited outside the Ostergrens' house while Brown changed into his new bicycling suit.

When he came outside pushing his wheel, her heart felt like it started dancing a hornpipe inside her chest. She couldn't take her eyes off his legs.

"What do you think?" Brown asked proudly. He turned around to give her the full effect.

The day suddenly seemed very warm indeed, and Kitty wished she had a fan with her. "You look very fine, Dr. Brown." Her heart continued dancing.

"Thanks to your excellent needlework!" He smiled broadly at her. "Give credit where it's due!"

Kitty blushed.

Brown nodded towards the road, indicating they should start walking. Together they moved away from the Ostergrens' house. "Thank you for saving me back there," Brown told Kitty. "If there's anything worse than Mrs. Ostergren's cooking, I'm sure I don't know what it is. At least her husband is a decent fellow. But, do you know, she uses fish skins to clear the coffee? Fish skins!" He pulled a wry face.

Kitty laughed, then said without thinking, "You should get a wife to save you from boarding house food!" After the words were out of her mouth she stopped suddenly, realizing what she'd said.

Brown stopped too, and looked at her a long moment. "I should," he agreed at last.

Kitty's eyes grew wide. Slowly, her chin tilted upwards. A lock of her golden hair had come loose and hung over her cheek; Brown reached up gently to brush it back.

Suddenly a loud trotting of hooves and clattering of harness burst upon them. "What in the Sam Hill is that thing?" Demanded a rough, twangy voice.

Kitty could have cried for disappointment at the breaking of such a tender moment. Brown —though not a man given to violence in ordinary circumstances— looked as though he wanted to knock the rider down.

The nature of the intruder made the interruption even worse, if that were possible. The rusty-saw accent proclaimed the identity of the local sawmill's foreman just as obviously as his scarred and dirty face.

"This, Bill Clapper—" Brown said, glaring upwards. "Is a fifty-two inch, nickel-plated Columbia bicycle!"

Bill snorted. "Whatever that means." Even over the smell of Bill's horse and harness, Brown could smell whiskey. They other man might be getting an extra-early start on inebriating himself before going back to work on Monday; more likely he'd been out all night on Saturday. He forced his horse offensively close to them and purposely jerked his reins to make the gelding protest as the metal bit dug into the animal's mouth.

Brown moved his bicycle protectively between Kitty and the agitated horse, using the Columbia's large driving wheel as a makeshift fence.

"I asked you a civil question." Clapper's tone was anything but civil, and his horse's ears moved nervously in response to his harsh tones. "There's no need to get all uppity! What are you doin' bringin' a thing like that on the road fer?"

Brown met Bill's gaze without flinching. "It's a public road," he said levelly. "I suppose I've got as much right to be here as you have."

"And what in the Sam Hill's you wearin', anyways?" Bill asked, ignoring Brown's statement and noticing his knickers for the first time. He continued to agitate his horse, jerking the reins and pushing the animal closer to the pedestrians than it wanted to be. The rough man gestured darkly at the gleaming bicycle. "You're gonna spook my horse with that thing."

Anger mingled with worry in Kitty's breast as Dr. Brown stood his ground. Anyone in Chetzemoka would have loved to see Bill Clapper bested, but the man had been a prize fighter before he'd let himself go to seed and gotten paunchy. He had three inches and at least sixty pounds on the doctor.

Kitty laid a soft hand on Brown's arm. "Elijah?"

In addressing Dr. Brown by his christian name, she instantly diverted his attention.

"Let's just go," she said gently.

His face softened as he met her pleading gaze. He nodded.

As they turned to go, Bill spit out a noxious stream of brown fluid. It hit the ground right by them, spattering Kitty's skirts.

Brown saw her blanch, then gag slightly. She glanced down, and the slightest trace of moisture appeared in her eyes

Brown's anger flared hotter than he would have ever thought possible and he moved forward to shield Kitty. Suddenly, he *needed* to beat Clapper —but he knew he'd never do it in a brawl.

He gently moved Kitty behind a nearby fence then jeered up at Bill, "Spook your horse? That old crowbait of yours wouldn't get excited if you lit a fire under him! In a race he'd be no match for my wheel!"

Bill colored, then guffawed. "Doc, yer dreamin'! You're sayin' yer gonna *ride* that there thing?"

Brown's eyes narrowed. "Faster than you'll ever go."

Bill tightened his grip on his reins. "Prove it! I'll race ya right here and now! Through town, out around the sawmill, then back down Water Street and end at the saloon!"

"You've got yourself a race!" Brown leaped into his saddle and was off as soon as he spoke the words.

It was the first time Kitty had actually seen him ride the wheel, and as he whirled away she stared after him in awe.

Part of her had wondered, deep down, if it were really possible for the large machine to even stay upright without support. Her heart had believed Dr. Brown implicitly, but in her mind there lurked a cynical shadow of doubt which questioned whether she might be putting faith in a claim which defied the laws of physics. As Brown leaped into his saddle and flew down the hill, he became living, quicksilver proof of all that he had told her.

Bill's jaw dropped open and he gaped after the doctor, clearly forgetting for the moment that he was supposed to be racing the man on the wheel. His horse obviously had no intention of reminding him. Being left at last in peace, the animal stood very, very still.

The nickel-plated bicycle gleamed like silver in the bright sun. Its spokes sliced the air like thresher blades as the wheel ran all the way to the end of Lawrence Street and turned downhill.

The whirling wheel kept Bill mesmerized as long as it was in view. Only when it turned the corner did he remember that he was in a race which had just started. He swore, then spurred his horse. The much put-upon animal balked, and Bill lost precious time getting it under control.

The town of Chetzemoka was built on two levels, with uptown on a series of hills like rumpled blankets on a bed which was still airing. From the lowest of these a bluff dropped to the waterfront downtown like a bed's counterpane falling to the floor. The uptown and downtown were connected at two places: a long, steep road at the far northern end of Water Street, and a set of precarious wooden stairs by the fire-watch tower in the middle of the bluff. The riders would have to take the road.

Without waiting for Bill to regain control of his horse, Kitty ran to the fire tower to watch Brown racing along Water Street.

As soon as Brown challenged Bill he cursed himself for a fool. Even as he set his wheels whirring and threw every ounce of energy into his pumping calves, he feared he'd be in for defeat.

The Boston Wheelmen had told him of contests between wheel and horse where the bicycle emerged the victor; but those had all been exceedingly long races. The bicycle's main advantage was its rider's staying power. In short bursts of sheer speed, the horse always won.

The distance to the mill and back was a little over six miles. One of the Boston men had said that a man on a wheel could best the fastest horse in the world on any course over five, but Brown expected the statement had been an exaggeration —and he took for granted that it had referred to an experienced cyclist. He was still just barely getting a feel for his new bicycle.

He flew down the hill to Water Street without touching finger to brake. He kept expecting to hear Bill's horse thunder behind, then overtake him, but magically, mysteriously, he didn't. Brown had no time to consider why. All his attention was focused on his wheel and the road speeding underneath him.

By the time he reached the bottom of the hill, he was going faster than he'd thought was possible —and was convinced he was going to crash. He managed the sharp turn at the bottom of the hill by using the whole space of the road, and thanked his creator there wasn't anyone there to crash into.

From Kitty's vantage at the top of the bluff, trees blocked the hill descent. Brown came into her sight when he turned onto Water Street, legs pumping furiously at his pedals. The gleaming bicycle was like nothing she'd ever seen before, gliding swiftly along the road and flashing in the sunlight. It still seemed incredible to her that the machine could remain upright, still more so that it could travel in such a straight line and cover ground so quickly. Her heart thrilled as she saw Brown's progress.

To the north, she heard madly pounding hoofbeats.

On weekdays, Water Street was Chetzemoka's busiest thoroughfare. On a Sunday there were fewer people crowding the road, but still enough to make things hazardous for a new rider engaged in a mad dash upon a wheel. Brown's progress —arrow-straight at first— soon became impeded by all the boys, dogs, and other obstacles he had to swerve around. They didn't dart out of his way like they would have instinctively dodged a pounding horse, and as Brown swerved time and time to avoid them he ground his teeth, thinking what an advantage his swiftly approaching competitor would have here.

As Brown swerved and swooped along the road, boys and men stared open-mouthed at his amazing machine. He heard feminine shrieks of surprise, and hoarse masculine voices yelling oaths and questions.

Then he heard the pounding of Bill's horse behind him.

As the road cleared for the oncoming beast, Brown threw everything he had into his pedals.

At the end of Water Street as they passed out of town, the horse came abreast of, then overtook the bicyclist. Bill jeered at Brown as he passed, but Brown put a damper on his anger and channeled all his fire into his legs. He'd known the horse would overtake him in the short run. His only hope lay in outlasting the animal.

As the road to the mill stretched long and straight before them, the real question —the important question— rose up: Who would win the race?

Chapter V

Watching Water Street from the top of the bluff, Kitty clenched her fists in frustration as she saw all the obstacles impeding Brown's progress. Boys deliberately jumped in front of him. Motionless dogs slept on in the middle of the street as he flew towards them, or lazily sat up and started howling in place. Kitty wanted to howl, too —to shout at the fools to get out of the way. As Bill turned onto Water Street and thundered towards Brown on his wheel, Kitty's nails dug into her palms.

Soon trees and buildings blocked her view of the wheelman. She climbed swiftly up the ladder at the side of the fire tower to keep him in view as long as possible.

Meanwhile, people were wandering past Kitty's position on their way to the nearby church. They all gawked up at her hanging there on the fire tower, shock and astonishment painted plainly on their faces. She twisted her skirts tightly around her legs so no one could look up them, hung onto the ladder with her other hand, and kept her eyes firmly on the race.

Bill was beating his horse hard. *Could she hear the beast's panting? Or did she only imagine it?* He was gaining on Brown.

People called up to Kitty. "What are you doing up there, Mrs. Butler?" "Is there a fire?"

"No fire, you fools!" Kitty hissed down at them. "Leave me alone!" Her gaze stayed riveted on the race.

Bill was nearly up to Brown now, but a large wagon blocked the road. The large vehicle left only a hair's breadth of space. The slim bicycle slipped through the narrow passage like a fish through reeds, but there was no space for Bill's horse. The doctor rode on, gaining ground.

Bill made gestures so wild Kitty could tell he was swearing, even from her distant vantage point. His horse balked and shied. The combination of the wild man and the angry animal disturbed the cart horses. As their master struggled to control them, first they backed up the wagon, then pulled it across the street, blocking the road more effectively than ever.

Bill jerked his reins savagely and forced his horse to mount the wooden sidewalk, and the women and children standing there scattered shrieking. Bill thundered through the crowd as if they were no more than flock of terrified hens and bypassed the wagon, then leapt his horse back into the street.

He whipped the animal to a frenzied gallop, and was soon gaining again on Brown. As they passed from sight, Kitty feared her dear doctor would never win against the animal's enormous speed.

The church bells rang.

To watch the disappearing racers as long as possible, Kitty dropped her twisted skirts and held a hand over her eyes, straining her vision into the distance. As they vanished from even this extended view and the church bells finished ringing, she considered what to do.

She was desperate to see Dr. Brown as soon as he came back into town, to congratulate or —as she feared more likely— to console him. But, she had no idea how long it would take him to ride the challenged course. Until he came back, she was serving no one by making a spectacle of herself on the fire tower. She climbed down, wondering if she could skip church.

Under ordinary circumstances a manufactured headache would have been a convenient excuse. However, the whole town had just seen her hanging off the side of the watch tower like the figurehead on a ship's prow. The headache excuse lacked credibility, to say the least. She'd have enough explaining to do, as things already stood.

She wondered if she might at least rush home and change her soiled skirts, but the rooms she rented were at the far end of uptown. Arriving at church halfway through services would give people even more to talk about.

Seeing few good options, Kitty straightened her hat, put on a brave face, and walked boldly around the corner to the church.

Services hadn't started yet. The congregation was seated, but chattering wildly.

"Did you see that *thing*?"

"Who didn't?"

"What on Earth was it?"

"It's nothin' natural, I vum!"

"That can't ever have been Dr. Brown!"

"What the Dickens was he wearing?"

"Bill Clapper's up to his usual Sunday sacrilege —nearly ran me down!"

"I wouldn't have expected it of the doctor!"

"On a Sunday!

"Really, what was that *thing*?"

Thanks to Mrs. Ostergren's wagging tongue, the connection between Kitty and Brown's outlandish apparel was already known. As soon as she entered the church, the babble of conversation rose to feverish intensity. Kitty kept her eyes level, and sat down in a dignified manner in the pew closest to the door.

When the minister mounted the pulpit, he looked appalled to find his congregation ignoring him as they kept up their excited gossip. He tried clearing his throat, but the hubbub continued. He looked from face to face, but everyone was too distracted to notice —except Kitty. When she — out of the whole congregation— met his eyes dutifully, he pursed his lips and gave her an Old-Testament look that made her wonder if he'd seen her position on the tower a few minutes earlier. Finally, to get everyone else's attention he had to tap the spine of his Bible against the lectern, like a judge rapping for order in a court.

When the church finally quieted, Reverend Curlew looked sternly out over the townsfolk. "Today's sermon," he announced gravely. "Is on the Eighth Commandment: Remember the sabbath day, to keep it holy."

By the way he looked straight at her as he announced the text, Kitty was fairly certain the minister *had* seen her hanging off the watch tower like a circus performer. On a Sunday. *Oh, dear...*

Reverend Curlew cleared his throat and commenced: "Since the primitive Christians instituted the first day of the week and the memorial of our Lord's resurrection as the day specially devoted to the services of the Almighty, it is our bounden duty to see that we observe the day with becoming reverence..."

Half the congregation turned to stare at Kitty. She shrank down in her pew seat.

Curlew had clearly had a variety of different individuals in mind when he'd written his sermon. When he spoke of the particular importance of avoiding sinful occupation on the Lord's day, he gave a hard look to a group of women in especially fine clothes. Kitty knew they called themselves seamstresses, but she had absolutely no worries they would ever compete with her dress shop for customers. When the reverend sermonized staring straight at them, they declined to look uncomfortable.

Curlew expanded on his theme at great length, then turned a page in his sermon. "Furthermore—" He looked out over his audience and stared hard at selected individuals: a few men in their work clothes, Kitty in her wrinkled and soiled skirts. "I hope at church you have on your best apparel. I shall wear no better dress at the wedding than when I come to the marriage of the King's Son. If I am well clothed on other occasions, I will be in the House of God. However reckless I may be about my personal appearance at other times, when I come into a consecrated assemblage I shall have on the best dress I have—"

At this inopportune moment Dr. Brown entered the church, still clad in his cycling knickers and carrying his cap.

"—We all understand the proprieties of everyday life and the proprieties of Sabbath life," said Reverend Curlew, then he saw Brown. He blanched, and lost his place in his text.

Total silence fell over the church.

Everyone in the congregation turned to see what had so discomfited their minister. Seeing Brown, they stared open-mouthed.

Besides being the only male in the church over the age of twelve who was wearing short-pants, Brown was covered in sweat. His left side was streaked with dirt, especially on the shoulder of his jacket, and his left stocking was torn.

A few children started whispering. Instead of shushing them, their mothers began speaking together in low voices behind hands and fans. Then the fathers joined the discussion in tones which they took even less pains to keep quiet.

Seeing all eyes upon him, Dr. Brown gave a sheepish grin and bowed his head towards the minister. He tried to act casual as he sat down next to Kitty in the pew closest to the door.

The juxtaposition of Dr. Brown and Mrs. Butler reminded everyone of her odd performance on the watch tower earlier that morning. It also reminded them all of what Mrs. Ostergren had said about Kitty's role in creating Brown's garments.

People gave up their attempts to keep quiet and the noise level in the church rose until it could have competed with a theater during intermission.

Reverend Curlew's face went from shocked pallor to a bright red rivaling the costliest of rubies. He tapped the lectern with his Bible for attention as he'd done at the start of the sermon. Then struggled to find his place in his notes again.

"We all understand the proprieties of everyday life and the proprieties of Sabbath life," he repeated, then expanded on the theme.

At first people kept glancing backwards at Brown and Kitty. After the minister had been droning on for some time though, people's necks started to get sore and they faced the pulpit again. Notwithstanding this, Kitty felt like they continued to watch her with eyes in the backs of their heads.

As soon as she had a chance to do so discretely, Kitty took the Bible from the back of the pew in front of her. She turned to Psalms, then caught Brown's eye. She pointed at Psalms 106:17: "The earth opened and swallowed up Dathan, and covered the company of Abiram."

Compared to sitting through this sermon, Kitty was inclined to think Dathan and Abiram's fate had been a relatively merciful one.

Brown gave Kitty a reassuring expression, and patted her hand under the Book. When no one else was looking he took the Bible from her and flipped to Exodus. He pointed at 15:1 and by his finger Kitty read, "I will sing unto the LORD, for he hath triumphed gloriously: the horse and his rider he has thrown into the sea."

Curlew's sermon went on much longer than usual, and Kitty could barely sit still through the rest of it. *Just how literal was the doctor being when he chose that quotation in Exodus? Did he really win? Bill didn't really get thrown into Puget Sound, did he?* She itched with curiosity.

The instant the sermon concluded, Brown and Kitty took advantage of their place by the door. They rushed outside ahead of everyone else. Brown's wheel was propped up by the church door; he grabbed it and ran hand-in-hand with Kitty towards her lodgings on Clallam Street.

As soon as they were out of earshot of the congregation, Kitty started laughing at how like two errant school children they seemed. *Even down to the knickers!* She thought, and laughed all the more merrily. Brown joined in, and between running and laughter they were both soon out of breath.

Gasping —and still laughing— Kitty looked around for somewhere they could catch their breath. At the top of one of the uptown hills was a large weeping willow. Brought by an early ship on Chetzemoka's trade route, the fast-growing tree was already full size; its branches hung to the ground and created a full curtain. Kitty pulled Brown into this natural bower. He set his wheel against the tree's trunk and they collapsed against each other until their hysterical laughter calmed down to giggles, then to soft sighs.

The summer sun shone through the willow's green leaves and dappled their private hideaway in tones of green and gold. As Kitty looked up into Elijah's eyes and their lips met, they were in shadows —and in sunlight.

Chapter VI

Kitty shared a suite of rented rooms with the town schoolteacher. Miss Bray was taking advantage of the summer recess to visit her relatives in Seattle, so Kitty and Brown had the rooms to themselves when they retreated there.

Brown borrowed an old floor rag to clean his bicycle before he brought it inside. As he wiped down his wheel Kitty went in ahead of him, glad of the opportunity to finally change her dress.

As she laid aside her soiled skirt, it occurred to Kitty that Brown was still covered in dried sweat and dirt from the race. For his own comfort (and for the sake of the nice furniture in her sitting room) she realized she should offer to let him get cleaned up before they sat down together.

The idea made her look around her bedroom with fresh eyes. She'd left the bed airing that morning with the bedclothes thrown back. Her spare corset was hanging over the rear of a chair; and in one corner of the room a cotton shift and a pair of pantelettes lay together in a rumpled heap where she'd tossed them to await laundry day.

Kitty rushed around the room setting these things to rights. Then she checked that there was water in the ewer, swiped a dust-cloth over her wash-stand and switched out the towel hanging on the wall for a fresh one before going back out to meet the doctor.

Brown had brought his bicycle in and leaned it against the inside of the door to avoid scratching the wallpaper. He stood near it, cap in hand, waiting expectantly for Kitty.

Seeing him again, Kitty found herself just as hard-pressed to avoid staring at his legs as she had earlier that morning. She forced herself to meet his eyes though, and held the door of her bedroom wide open. "Would you like to get washed up?" She pointed at the marble-topped stand in the corner, where soap and a sponge were arranged near her washbasin and ewer.

Brown looked into the cozy feminine room, at the pretty china bowl and pitcher painted with roses even pinker than the ones which bloomed in Kitty's cheeks. The invitation to enter this sanctuary made his heart thump harder than it had during the race he'd ridden that morning. He swallowed as his mouth went dry, then nodded and thanked her.

Just as he was turning to go into the room, a thought occurred to Kitty. "Oh, wait!" She called, halting him. "Come over here by the window and wait a minute."

Startled at this sudden change, he turned to follow her directions and was surprised when she swept past him into her room.

She came back out immediately with a clothes-brush in her hand. "Here," she instructed. "Hold still for me."

He obeyed and she started vigorously brushing the dirt out of his jacket. Brown laughed.

"You're making me feel like a horse being curried!" He quipped.

Kitty stopped abruptly, and Brown was sure he must have said something wrong. She looked at the clothes brush with a sad expression. Brown cursed himself for distressing her, but was utterly perplexed as to what he'd done.

"What is it?" He asked earnestly. "What's wrong?"

She went back to brushing his jacket, more slowly and thoughtfully this time. "My late husband used to say that," she told him at last. "When I'd do this for him."

"I'm sorry, I—"

"It's alright." She interrupted his apology, moving down from Brown's shoulder where she'd started and brushing the dirt from his elbow. "You didn't know."

She shook out the brush then ran her fingers through its bristles before continuing. "He did surveying for the railroads. It's dusty work."

She looked away sadly. Her eyes followed the dust she'd shaken from the brush as it swirled in the sunbeams coming through the window, then fell to the ground.

"The railroad company sent him out here," she continued. "He was so certain they were going to put a line through to Chetzemoka!" She sighed. "We had sort of a whirlwind romance, and then he was gone surveying so much—" She shook her head. When she went on her words were very quiet, as though she were speaking to herself. "I always told myself we'd have a whole lifetime to get to know each other, but then he died so soon and so sudden, sometimes I feel like I hardly knew him at all. Afterwards, it almost felt like I was more in mourning for that lost chance to really know him, than I was for the man himself."

She started, realizing she'd spoken these words aloud. "Does that shock you?" She asked, meeting Brown's eyes.

The doctor shook his head. "It's no more than I've heard from every mother of a stillborn child, or of one that died in infancy," he told her gently. "It's natural."

She was quiet a moment. Then she confided, "I always told myself that if I fell in love again, I'd do my hardest to learn everything I could about him from the very first, that I'd learn all I could about the things he enjoyed from the very start of things." As she said it, her eyes moved involuntarily towards the bicycle leaning against the door.

Brown saw the direction of her glance, and he smiled. He tilted Kitty's chin up so she would meet his eyes. "I think that's something any man worth your attention would be pleased to hear."

She smiled and moved to lay her head on his shoulder. A whiff of his sharp, sweaty scent dispelled her sober mood and she drew back giggling. "You smell like a mule!" She chided, pushing him away and pointing towards her room. "Go get washed up!"

When Brown came back out (smelling of lavender soap now), there were two tumblers of lemonade and a plate of home-made taffy arranged on a small table in the sitting room. Kitty had her work basket next to her on a long chair and was threading a needle. "Give me that torn stocking," she ordered matter-of-factly.

He obediently complied, then felt slightly awkward sitting there with one shoe on and one bare foot. "Now," Kitty said, pinching the edges of the split together. "Tell me how the race went! I saw you go down Water Street—" She told him how she'd climbed up the fire tower to watch and been seen hanging there by the whole town.

Brown laughed with her over it and helped her see the humor in Reverend Curlew's consternation.

Then she urged him to finish the story for her. "I'm itching to know what happened after you left town!"

He stretched his legs and started massaging his calves. "Bill's horse got quite a ways ahead of me at first, but I knew he'd tire himself out pretty quick. I figured if I could outlast him, I'd start having a chance once the animal got winded."

"Do you think the poor horse will be alright?" Kitty asked, concern touching her tender nature.

"Oh, that horse will be just fine!" Brown assured her, smirking. "But Bill's going to need a new hat —and possibly some new boots."

Kitty gave him a quizzical look and he continued. "I was already catching up when we got near the sawmill, and by the time we reached it we were neck-in-neck again. I was still feeling pretty strong and I figured I could beat Bill on the run back to town. Then his horse decided to give me some help." He laughed, remembering the scene. "That animal must have figured the reason Bill was in such an all-fired hurry was because he was late for work! It slowed down and stopped as soon as they got to the mill door!"

Kitty joined in Brown's laughter.

"But what was it you were saying about a hat —and boots?" She asked again when they'd stopped giggling.

"Well," he went on with the story. "I kept going so I didn't exactly see what happened next, but it doesn't take much imagination to guess Bill wasn't too happy about things. And any animal Bill owns is liable to get just as ornery as him, out of self-defense if for no other reason! I looped the mill, like Bill said at the start of the race, and when I came back around the horse had thrown him into the millpond!"

Kitty tried not to laugh, but she really couldn't avoid chuckling. Brown continued: "I'm afraid I let it make me a little cocky —and, well, you know what the preachers say about pride." He looked wryly at his sleeve. Kitty had managed to brush out most of the dirt, although a slight shadow remained which would take washing to remove completely.

"You had a fall?" Kitty asked, her eyes full of concern.

"Not a bad one," Brown assured her. "Going uphill I hit a rut in the road and went down. It's my own fault —I should have been paying more attention!"

Kitty shook her head. "It happens with horses all the time," she pointed out. "At least your bicycle didn't break its leg when it happened!"

Brown laughed. "True, true! Anyhow, by the time I was up and riding again, Bill was back in the game. It evidently hadn't taken him long to flounder back out of the millpond, and the bit of rest while he did must have done his horse some good. I had a hard time keeping ahead of them for a good two miles, but by the time we got near town again that horse was all run out and nothing Bill did could make it go faster than a walk. I put on all the speed I could and came to the finish with them far behind me."

Kitty set the stocking in her lap and beamed at him. "I'm so proud of you!" Brown basked in the sunshine of her smile.

They drank in the expressions in each other's eyes a long moment. Then Kitty concentrated on the mending in her lap again and commented, "I'll bet Bill Clapper's fit to be tied!"

"Oh my, yes!" Brown laughed. "When he got into town and saw me waiting there on the street in front of the saloon, he looked like he couldn't decide whether to knock me down or shoot me! I figured church was the safest place in town I could be for the next few hours —even though I was late, and in quite a state!"

Kitty shook her head, trying to keep a straight face. "What a sermon for today! For both of us!"

Brown tried to look appropriately contrite, but a smile played at the corners of his lips. "Can you imagine Reverend Curlew ever considering a bicycle of his own, like the minister at my cousin's church in Boston?"

Kitty's eyes went wide. When she contemplated the picture of stern and gangly old Reverend Curlew astride a wheel like Brown's, even respect for the man's office couldn't keep her from giggling.

They lingered over their candy and lemonade. Kitty returned Brown's freshly mended stocking, and after replacing his shoe he assured her he couldn't even see her repair. She flushed with pleasure at the compliment and with pride in her work. Again, Brown reflected how much her cheeks reminded him of roses.

He wanted to ask if he could start walking her home from work in the evenings, but he knew the unpredictability of his profession would surely interfere with such a regular personal commitment. When emergencies arose —and they so often did— he couldn't deny his patients, but he didn't want to leave Kitty waiting either.

He settled for asking if he could walk her to church the next Sunday. When she smiled sweetly and answered that she'd like that, his heart swelled bigger than a balloon.

Before Brown left Kitty's rooms, they kissed again —more shyly than they had under the willow. For all its timidity though, their kiss this time seemed to mark the beginning of something as beautiful as a rainbow.

Chapter VII

The next morning Kitty's most lucrative customer walked into her dress shop only a few minutes after she'd unlocked the door. The woman met Kitty's warm welcome with a stern look, informed her that she was cancelling her most recent order, and departed so quickly that Kitty didn't even have time to ask for a reason.

After a moment of stunned shock, Kitty shook her head and brought out her accounts book. A worried frown creased her brow. The cancelled order had been an elaborate carriage dress and the fabrics had just come in. If she couldn't find some other customer who wanted them, it would be a tight squeeze for her to make rent at the end of the month.

I'm sure I can find one or two buyers for the four yards of brocade, Kitty said to herself. *But who in this town will take sixteen yards of peacock green silk on a whim?*

She shook her head, then ran her eyes down her customer list, contemplating (and rejecting) various options.

Mrs. A. can't afford it. Miss B. hates green. Mrs. C. just went from second mourning to half mourning for her husband's grandfather, and by the time she goes into colors again we'll be halfway through fall ...

Kitty had reached this point in her list when the bell over the shop door rang. She looked up and saw a young woman wearing a neatly pressed calico dress. She stepped inside the shop and stopped just past the door, fidgeting nervously with a handkerchief she held in both hands.

"Good morning, Miss Johnson!" Kitty welcomed her. "Is everything alright?"

Miss Johnson's lower lip trembled slightly. "Mrs. Butler—" she began, then stopped. She pressed her lips together, looked quickly up at the ceiling, then closed her eyes a moment before starting again. "Mrs. Butler, I'm sorry. I'm afraid I have to cancel my wedding dress order with you."

Kitty gasped. "Good heavens! Has something happened to young Mr. Dunn?"

"Oh, Ezra's fine!" Miss Johnson assured Kitty quickly. "We're still getting married in October, nothing's changed there. It's just— The dress— My ma said—"

Miss Johnson paused to again stop herself from crying. The words which followed came out all in a rush. "Last night my ma told me she didn't want you to make the dress." Her eyes started streaming, and she scrubbed at them with her handkerchief.

Kitty guided her gently towards a chair. "Here. Here, sit down a minute. It's alright." She poured a glass of water from a pitcher she kept on a small table in the corner, and gently handed it to Miss Johnson. "The wedding's still on, that's what matters."

"I was *so* looking forward to that lovely dress we talked about!" The glass in her hands trembled so hard some of the water spilled out. "Just like the one in the fashion plate—"

"It's alright," Kitty insisted. She concentrated on reassuring Miss Johnson, and stamped down firmly on the part of her mind which rang alarm bells about what it meant to have another major order cancelled. "Did your mother say why?"

Miss Johnson drained the water glass and placed it on the floor. Then she stiffened, set her jaw and looked away. "We saw you before church yesterday, and then we heard what everyone was saying about you making those— whatever it was Dr. Brown was wearing." She stood, still looking away.

Miss Johnson glared at the wall a long moment, then set her jaw. "Afterwards Ma said it was bad luck to have a widow make a bridal gown." She hurried out of the shop then, not meeting Kitty's eyes.

Kitty's blood ran cold at the young woman's parting words. She reached for the chair Miss Johnson had just vacated and sat down heavily. Her legs felt like they were shaking too badly to support her.

She was still reeling when Mrs. Snow thundered in to complain how gravely insulted she'd felt when she'd seen the material originally intended for her equestrian dress repurposed as knickers for a grown man. Kitty pointed out the equestrian suit had been cancelled, and as Mrs. Snow had never paid for the fabric Kitty was entitled to do anything she liked with it. This simply raised Mrs. Snow to an even greater level of indignation, and as she thundered out of the shop her skirts knocked over a wastepaper basket, a stack of fashion magazines, and the water glass Miss Johnson had left on the floor.

No one else came into the shop all morning, and the few who did come by in the early afternoon had more cancellations to make. The strain gave Kitty a nervous headache. By early afternoon, she felt as though a blacksmith were hammering inside her skull.

She closed shop early and borrowed some extra veiling material from her own backstock. She draped three thicknesses of veil over her face to mitigate the effects of the sun on her headache, then locked up and headed towards Dr. Brown's office.

His door was ajar, and his bicycle leaned on the wall inside. The army-style canvas doctor's roll Kitty had made for him was attached to the handlebars by two leather straps that held it firm but would be lightning-quick to open if needed. The steed of steel seemed ready to speed off to any emergency.

Kitty didn't knock: she want to subject her splitting head to any more noise than was absolutely necessary. She listened for voices beyond the partway open door; then, hearing nothing, walked gingerly inside.

Dr. Brown was seated at a sturdy maple desk, frowning at an accounts ledger. He heard Kitty's light step and looked up. "Mrs. Butler!"

Kitty was pleased that he recognized her, even though he couldn't possibly make out much of her face through the thick veils. Most men couldn't even remember the main colors of a woman's dress, let alone their clothing's details. She wondered if —just perhaps— Dr. Brown had been studying her figure closely enough to recognize her that way. The thought sent delightful electric tingles all through her body, but the blacksmith kept pounding away inside her skull. She said as quietly as she could manage, "I was hoping you might have something for a headache."

Dr. Brown looked surprised, but he nodded and took action immediately. His right hand opened a glass-fronted cupboard and took out one of the larger vials in it, and his left hand simultaneously closed the curtain above his desk.

He carefully measured a dose of headache powder from the vial into a drinking glass and added water, then added some drops shaken from a smaller bottle. Even standing several paces away, Kitty could tell by the smell that the smaller bottle contained lavender water. Dr. Brown swirled the glass in a fast circle until the powder dissolved so he wouldn't make noise by stirring it, then handed the mixture to Kitty and told her to drink it slowly.

The lavender helped cover the headache powder's bitter taste of feverfew and willow bark. As Kitty took her medicine, Dr. Brown moved with silent speed around the room, closing the other curtains to block out the sunlight. Grateful for this consideration, Kitty removed her veils and hat. She closed her eyes in the dark room, hoping the mixture would work quickly.

Dr. Brown gently took Kitty's veils, hat and hatpins, then softly suggested she let down her hair from its chignon.

Her eyes flew open and her heart beat fast. Dr. Brown saw her nervous look and gave her a small, soothing smile. "It's alright," he assured her. "Here, there's a cot in the corner. Just let your hair down and come lie down on your back."

The blacksmith pounding at the inside of Kitty's skull was joined by another hammering in her chest. She suddenly wondered why she hadn't just gone to the druggist and bought headache powder for herself. No one bothered a doctor for a trivial thing like a headache. No wonder Dr. Brown had looked surprised when she told him why she'd come! She didn't really know the whole reason herself.

Kitty perched on the edge of the cot and tried to remember the last time she had been treated by a doctor. *It must have been back in Ohio before I was married*, she realized. *The time I had scarlet fever as a teenager.*

She took a long, full breath as she reached up towards her chignon. Her hands shook. This might have been easier if she were the sort of woman who splurged on a hairdresser from time to time, but she'd always considered such things a waste of money. Only one man had seen her hair down and loose since she'd been a grown woman, and that had been her husband.

"You can take your shoes off, if you like," Dr. Brown told her, still speaking very quietly out of consideration for her headache. "I keep a spare buttonhook in my desk that you can use to put them back on again before you leave."

Kitty drew her hands away from her hair, grateful for the suggestion. Her head was still pounding, but it was...hard to take her hair down in front of Dr. Brown. Despite his professional demeanor, despite the office.

Perhaps it was especially hard *because* of these things. She suddenly wished she could have shown him her hair for the first time in different circumstances, and shown it to him not as Doctor Brown, but as Elijah.

Boots were easier. She reached down and deftly flicked gutta percha buttons out of the buttonholes curving around her ankles. Then she slipped her feet out of her boots and pulled her legs up onto the cot. It was done in less than a minute, and part of her wished she'd forced herself to be a little slower about it.

Her fingers trembled as she slid her hairpins, one by one, from her coiled golden hair. She kept her gaze averted, turned towards the desk. She didn't trust herself to watch Dr. Brown's expression as her hair came loose. She wasn't even sure what she would have hoped to see there. Clinical detachment, like the good doctor he was? Or the look she would have longed to see in Elijah's eyes the first time she shared the intimacy of her hair with him, if only she'd thought things through? Again, she wondered why she'd come here. She didn't regret coming —not exactly— but nor did she comprehend her own motivations.

Her hair uncoiled into a long, loose question mark. She lay down on the cot and closed her eyes.

"Just relax," Dr. Brown told her. He sat down very quietly in a chair by the head of the cot. He reached forward and very gently cradled Kitty's head in his hands. She felt as though a deep peace flowed from his fingertips, and as he held her that way, she could feel her muscles relaxing, from her scalp all the way to her toes.

Very slowly, Dr. Brown gently drew his fingers apart and let Kitty's head rest delicately upon the cot. Then he slowly cradled it in his hands again, and again gently let it go.

He did this a number of times, always with the same gentle slowness. His strong hands would cup the curves at the base of her skull, the places which phrenologists call the bumps of amativeness. Then he would slowly draw his hands apart and lay her down again. He seemed to be carrying away her headache on his fingertips.

Kitty sighed, and slowly relaxed. She thought of how her day had gone, and finally understood why she had sought out Elijah when everything seemed so bleak. Somehow, she had just known that being near him would make things better.

Chapter VIII

When Mrs. Butler's deep, even breathing told the doctor his patient had fallen asleep, he gently uncurled his fingertips from the occiput of her skull. He carefully tucked a pillow under her head and covered her with a blanket. Then he placed his buttonhook on the floor next to her boots, for when she woke up.

Kitty had never come to him as a patient before. Since she had done so that day, he tried hard to just think of her as Mrs. Butler. But seeing her sleeping so peacefully there, with her golden hair all around her like an enchanted princess in a fairy tale, it was very, very hard to forget that this was Kitty. Hard not to look at her beautiful rosebud lips and remember how they'd felt against his when he'd kissed her just the day before.

He lifted a medical journal from the top of his desk. He quietly took the magazine and a chair outside, then sat himself near his office door.

He read a long article on President Garfield's condition after the recent assassination attempt, then a few shorter pieces—one discussing quinine's potential in epilepsy treatment, and another discussing milk indigestion.

The dry articles helped distract him from Kitty at least, but he had other things on his mind. He set the journal down in his lap and frowned out over the street.

Earlier in the day a number of women (mothers of large families) had come by his office and told him they no longer desired his services. When Mrs. Butler came by he'd been going over his accounts book determining just how many patients he had left. When he'd heard the light footsteps of a woman entering his office, he'd worried it was yet another matron come to tell him she didn't want him near her family. He'd been unspeakably relieved when he'd looked up and seen it was Kitty.

He'd recognized her right away, despite the heavy veils hiding her face. Her exquisite figure and graceful movements declared her identity in a way beyond question. He would have recognized Kitty Butler if all he'd seen of her had been her silhouette through a curtain.

There I am, thinking of her again, he realized. He smiled to himself. *Well, I suppose that's not really such a bad thing.*

He wondered if she would sleep long. A nap would help her headache, and as far as his office was concerned, it probably wouldn't matter if she was there all afternoon. Everyone who had appointments with Dr. Brown that day had already cancelled them. He tried to concentrate on his medical journal again.

Dr. Brown had ridden his bicycle to work, and stayed in his cycling suit after he'd reached his office. If any emergency arose or someone sent a messenger requesting a house call, his wheel was the fastest way to get to a patient. This had been in his mind all the time he'd been saving for a bicycle. It could go faster than a horse and buggy, and would be able to take him over some roads and short cuts which a horse couldn't pass. The bicycle could go night and day without tiring — something no horse could ever do. Besides all that, he'd never have to lose time hitching it. Under some circumstances, the few extra minutes spent hitching a buggy could mean the difference between life and death to a patient.

From the first time Brown had seen bicycles in Boston, he'd immediately comprehended how useful such a machine would be a physician. Now he wondered why no one else seemed to see the things which were so obvious to him.

A woman walked past Brown on the wooden sidewalk. At her side trotted a young boy, sucking on a green and yellow boiled sweet. Dr. Brown smiled at them, and the woman looked away disapprovingly. Her son, on the other hand, stopped in his tracks. He stared at Dr. Brown's cycling knickers, looked down at his own short-pants, then stared back at Dr. Brown again.

"Good afternoon," Dr. Brown said pleasantly.

The boy looked up at his mother. He took the boiled sweet out of his mouth and pointed at Dr. Brown with it, then shook the candy at his knickers. The mother grabbed her son's hand and hurried him away, her skirts swishing loudly.

Dr. Brown sighed, then consulted his watch. His bicycling outfit didn't include a waistcoat, since a vest would have restricted his movements and made it impossible to ride his machine. The watch pocket in his bicycling suit was small, and located on the outside of his jacket. He'd taken his long, dangling watch chain off of his timepiece and replaced it with a much shorter, more delicate, chain. This one was barely a few inches from one end to the other; the Boston Wheelmen had given it to him as a parting gift. Instead of being elaborately counterweighted with various fobs as in the traditional watch chain arrangement, this short little chain simply had a strong clip on the end which attached directly to the pocket.

Opening his watch's hunter case, Brown saw that he'd been outside longer than he'd realized. It was near the end of his office hours, and he had an appointment to make a house call on cranky old Silas Hayes.

He gently opened his office door and checked on Mrs. Butler. She was awake. She sat perched on the edge of the cot, buttoning her boots. Her hair was already back up in its chignon.

"How's your head?" Dr. Brown asked softly.

She looked up and smiled at him. "Much better, thank you."

She looked away and unconsciously raised a hand towards her hair. It was all neatly pinned in place, yet her fingers ran in a curve around her ear as though tucking away a stray lock. When she looked back at Dr. Brown and saw him watching her she seemed embarrassed. She let her hand fall, then went back to fastening her boots.

When she was finished, she stood up and handed the buttonhook to Dr. Brown with a thoughtful expression. She paused, then reached

80

up towards the back of her head. "What you did—" She traced her fingertips across the base of her skull. "Back here?" The expression in her voice and eyes made it a question.

"Part of something called the Swedish Movement Cure," Brown explained. "It was one of the most relaxing parts of medical school, I can assure you."

Since he'd come into the office Mrs. Butler's expression had been far away and sleepy. The word "Swedish" seemed to remind her of something though, and she became more alert. "Dr. Brown? What would you say to a decently cooked dinner, for a change? I'm sure it's not prideful to say that I can do a better job than Mrs. Ostergren."

Dr. Brown laughed. "No, there is nothing prideful in that statement at all!" He assured her. "Nor is there the slightest doubt in my mind that you are a much better cook than my landlady."

Kitty laughed at the conviction in his tone. She folded her veils and tucked the silk net away in her purse as they discussed a time for dinner at her rooms. Then she put her hat on and departed, smiling shyly over her shoulder at Dr. Brown as she went out the door.

Chapter IX

As he rode up the hill to Silas Hayes' mansion, Dr. Brown shuddered to think of how the foul-tempered old man would react to his bicycling suit. He briefly considered going home first to change clothes, then walking to Hayes' place. He didn't have time for that, though. Besides, if the bicycle was going to be his usual vehicle on his rounds (and that *was* still Dr. Brown's plan), Mr. Hayes would see his riding suit sooner or later. Brown might as well find out today how the old man would respond to it.

I wonder if he'll also tell me he doesn't want my services any more, like so many other people today. It was a sobering thought.

Silas Hayes was Brown's most regular source of income. He demanded the doctor make lengthy house calls several times a week, despite there really being nothing medically wrong with him. Whenever Brown started to feel guilty about taking money from someone whose maladies were all in his head, he reminded himself that the only way Hayes could get anyone to endure his unpleasant company for more than five minutes at a stretch was to pay them to do so. If he did send Brown away, the doctor worried the old man might finally go into a real decline —from loneliness.

Brown was apprehensive as he rode up to Hayes mansion. He carefully placed his bicycle on the porch, unstrapped his canvas medical roll from the handlebars, and rang the doorbell.

The new nurse answered the door. Brown was unsurprised by this, but it was not encouraging.

"Housekeeper gone?" He asked.

"Yes, Dr. Brown."

"Did she leave on her own, or did he fire another one?"

"Dr. Brown, he told *me* to fire her."

Brown cringed.

She went on, "I told him such a thing had nothing to do with my duties as a trained nurse — a *trained nurse*, Dr. Brown—" She repeated the phrase, giving Brown a steely glare. "And he threw his bowl of panada at me! It's one thing that he'd had me re-make that panada three separate times —first he said there was too much nutmeg in it, then the cracker crumbs were too fine, then—"

"I understand—" Brown broke in, using his most placatory tone.

"But to throw it at me! Not that it hasn't happened before —I've had my share of hard patients. But Dr. Brown, for him to expect a trained nurse to fire his housekeeper for him, as if I were his wife—"

"It's unreasonable, I agree—" Brown tried to head off what he knew was coming next.

"If he can't get it through his head soon what a nurse does and does not do, I'll be on the next steamer for Seattle, and no mistake!" She paused for breath.

Then she took a step backwards, looking Brown up and down. She had evidently just noticed his cycling knickers for the first time. "Dr. Brown, what on Earth are you wearing?"

Before he could reply, Hayes' voice came bawling down the stairs. "Nurse! Nurse! The sun moved! You need to shut the other side of the curtains again!"

The nurse cast her gaze heavenwards.

"I'll deal with him," Dr. Brown promised. "Go for a walk and get some fresh air."

The nurse sighed gratefully. "Thank you, Dr. Brown."

They moved past each other, the nurse going outside as Brown came in. The sound of her leather shoes on the wooden porch told him that she turned and paused as soon as she passed him. He didn't look back though, so he didn't know whether she had stopped to stare at his bicycle — or at his legs.

He took a deep breath and headed upstairs.

As he pushed open the door to Mr. Hayes' room, Brown thought he was prepared for anything. As it turned out, he was prepared for anything *except* what actually happened.

Mr. Hayes did not ask Brown if had taken leave of his senses. He didn't ask if Brown was unaware that he was a grown man, or if he was on his way to a costume party. Silas Hayes simply took one look at Brown and asked, "Is that what you're wearing now?"

Brown replied in the affirmative, and Hayes nodded. That was all. Then he ordered Brown to adjust the curtains, take away two of his blankets, and to look at a spot he was absolutely certain must be a terrible cancer which would kill him in six months.

Dr. Brown examined the spot on Mr. Hayes skin and assured him it was only a pimple. Then he adjusted the curtains according to Mr. Hayes' exacting specifications. By the time he'd satisfied the old man, the curtains were exactly one-eighth of an inch to the left of where they'd started. Finally he undraped two of Hayes' blankets and set them within easy reach of his bed, knowing Hayes would want one or both of them again within ten minutes.

Hayes seemed disappointed to hear that his suspected cancer was only a pimple. He consoled himself with a very long and detailed description of every single bowel movement he'd had since last seeing the doctor. As usual, he had taken detailed notes in a small diary. Silas Hayes was the only man Dr. Brown had ever met who kept a journal for his colon. Brown listened patiently, answering Hayes' questions and offering reassurances when needed.

After nearly an hour of this Hayes finally exhausted his topic and put away his colon diary. He went on to reminisce about his efficiency as a contracts lawyer before he'd retired. "By golly, I could negotiate more contracts in a day than you could shake a stick at..."

Brown pretended interest while examining the latest accumulation of patent medicines on Hayes dresser. Every door-to-door peddler of quack remedies in Jefferson County knew that Silas Hayes was an easy mark, and Dr. Brown always made a point of checking through the latest additions. As Hayes talked, the doctor divided the bottles into two groups: harmless and unadvised.

"—And I read every single word in every single contract thoroughly. Thoroughly, mind you! I was never one of those fools who thought just because he'd known a man twenty years he could trust that man enough to sign a contract from him without reading the fine print! Take that fool brother-in-law of mine—"

Brown pulled the cork out of a bottle and sniffed at its contents. *Ginger root, sage, and molasses*, he determined. *That won't hurt him.* He re-stoppered the bottle and set it down with the "harmless" group.

"That fool my sister married—" Hayes continued, "—was doing alright until he was idiot enough to stand security for his cousin without reading the fine print. If he'd asked me, I could have told him—"

Brown sniffed at another bottle. *Ginseng and licorice root. That one might actually do him some good.* He put it at the front of the harmless group.

"—That a man's a fool who thinks he can trust people without reading fine print!"

Brown nodded, and used a tiny corkscrew to open another bottle. As soon as the cork popped out he didn't even need to bring it near his nose to tell what was in it. *About three cents' worth of moonshine, in a half-dollar bottle.* He put it with the other group. Then he checked through

Hayes' collection of unguents and liniments to make sure none of them had gone rancid.

Hayes continued: "The whole mess put him in debt so far that I'm sure he'll never get out of it. If that fool thinks I'm going to provide for his son —even if the boy is my sister's child— well, then—"

Dr. Brown suggested that Hayes was in danger of agitating himself to an unhealthy degree. At this news the old man's eyes widened and he immediately ceased commentary on the economic woes of his sister's family. He drew out a gold-plated, eighteen-jewel repeater watch and spent the next two minutes in utter silence while he measured his own pulse.

Brown spent the time writing out dosages for Hayes latest harmless patent medicine acquisitions. The bottles he'd sorted into the other group were mostly cheap alcohol sold at exorbitant prices. He explained this to Hayes, and suggested the best use for them would be killing flies. This gave the old lawyer the notion to sue the snake-oil peddler who'd sold them to him. The thought put a rare smile on the curmudgeon's face.

Dr. Brown measured Hayes' pulse (regular), listened to his lungs (normal), and left his patient happily contemplating the prospect of prosecution.

Dr. Brown found the nurse outside, talking to Hayes' neighbor through the fence that separated their properties.

"Evenin' Doc!" Mr. Goldstein greeted him. "I hear Hayes is out another housekeeper!"

"I'm afraid so, Mr. Goldstein. Is there any chance your wife could fill in again, until he lines up another one?"

Goldstein rubbed his chin thoughtfully. "I'll ask her, Doc."

"You know Mr. Hayes would pay her well," Brown pointed out.

Goldstein laughed. "Well, Rachel wouldn't turn down the price of a new silk dress. You should see her staring at those fashion plates in the magazines, the way some men stare at fancy horses. I tell her she should have married a coal baron instead of a marine engineer." Goldstein's face grew more serious, in a gentle way. "Let's be honest though, Doc. Mr. Hayes is an old man with no friends, and he's driven off what little family he had. Last time Rachel took care of his place, she told me that no matter how much he paid her, working for him was less an employment and more of a *mitzvah*."

Brown gave Thompson a grateful smile. "Thank you —and please tell Mrs. Goldstein I said thanks, too."

Brown turned to the nurse. "Nurse, do you have a copy of that book of household management by the English woman? The one as long as a bible, with all the recipes?"

"Mrs. Beeton's book? Of course, Doctor. I have the latest edition."

"Good! Show Mr. Hayes the chapter on the duties of the sick nurse. Then show him the chapters on the duties of the housekeeper. He's an old contracts lawyer, and I guarantee he won't ask you to step out of your role again once he's seen it codified in a written document. Now then—" Brown checked his watch. "If you'll both excuse me, I have somewhere I need to be."

He turned his wheel towards Kitty's rooms, and wondered what she was cooking for dinner.

Chapter X

As soon as Kitty left Dr. Brown, she worried that she might have made a mistake in asking him to dinner. She desperately wanted to make a good impression. If she'd had a real kitchen at her disposal, it would have been relatively easy to make him think well of her cooking. However, real kitchens and rented rooms tend to be mutually exclusive.

The rooms Kitty shared with Miss Bray had only a small stove that gobbled nearly as much wood as a full-sized range yet put out a tiny fraction of a range's heat. It was never intended to be a cookstove; it was designed as a particularly cheap parlor stove. Whenever they tried to cook anything elaborate on it, something was sure to go wrong.

She fretted over the matter as she walked away from the doctor's office, second-guessed herself as she walked past the beach downtown where some Indian women were selling baskets, and chewed her lip as she followed the road uptown.

At least a salad is easy, Kitty reflected. *I still have some boiled peas and green beans in the ice box left over from dinner last night, so I can make a nice macedoine salad. As for meat, that horrid little stove of mine would never manage mock terrapin or timbale. Do I dare splurge on chicken, despite those cancelled orders this morning and no idea how I'm going to make up the lost income?*

She saw the butcher's door closing as she approached, and ran to get there before the business shut for the day. She arrived just as the butcher's wife was reaching for the "Open" sign. The woman gave Kitty a cold look through the window, turned the sign to "Closed," and smugly locked the door. Kitty turned away so the woman wouldn't have the satisfaction of seeing the angry tears that welled up in her eyes.

Well, now what do I do? She asked herself.

She walked all the way home without being able to think of a solution. When she got to her door she rummaged in her purse for her room keys, but found only the keys to her dress shop and realized she must have left the others at work. Cursing herself for the oversight, she returned downtown.

On her way back home she passed the same beach where the Indian women had been selling baskets earlier. They had evidently finished for the day: two canoes were pulled up to the shore, and a few Indian men were shifting aside fishing gear and the day's catch to make room for the women and their remaining baskets.

Kitty stopped, her attention arrested by the silver-scaled King salmon in the canoe. A raven-haired girl noticed her gaze and assumed she was looking at a large, elaborately woven basket that had just been placed next to the fish. The girl picked up the basket and carried it over to Kitty.

"Beautiful, isn't it?" The girl smiled pleasantly. "My grandmother made it." She called out a name, and a very old woman whose face was a mass of wrinkles came over to them. She smiled, assuming (like the girl) that Kitty was looking at the basket.

"It takes a lot of work to make a basket like this," the girl continued, persuasively working up to ask a price a commensurate with the work.

"Lot of work," the old woman agreed, still smiling at Kitty.

It was all such ordinary sales behavior, yet after the day she'd had Kitty was overwhelmed by the kindness of it. She was ashamed to admit that she wasn't shopping for a basket.

"Actually—" Kitty forced her next words out in a hurry. "—I was hoping to buy a piece of one of your fish." The statement rushed out in a low, embarrassed tone that was almost a mutter.

"Our fish?" The girl looked disappointed.

The grandmother hadn't caught what Kitty said, but she saw the girl's change of expression. She asked something sharply in the native language. The girl replied in the same tongue. The grandmother laughed and gained a confident expression. She said something condescending to her grand-daughter, and gave Kitty a friendly, understanding nod.

"Fish!" The old woman declared approvingly in English. "Which kind?"

"I'd like a piece of your salmon, please," Kitty said timidly and pointed.

"Salmon? Good choice!" The grandmother stepped over to the canoe and hauled out one of the salmon. It seemed to cost her no effort at all, even though the fish was almost as long as she was tall.

Kitty asked the grand-daughter to explain that she wanted a piece big enough for just two people.

Without waiting for a translation, the old woman nodded and went to work. In less time than it would have taken Kitty to simply gut the fish, two enormous fillets were laying on some kelp in front of her. Kitty reflected that the old woman seemed to have a different idea than she did about just how much salmon two people could eat, but the price the old woman asked was reasonable so she didn't quibble.

She carried the salmon home wrapped in the seaweed, holding it awkwardly away from herself in an attempt to avoid dripping anything on her dress. *At least it'll be easier to cook than chicken,* she reflected. *I think even that dreadful stove of mine can manage salmon.*

Chapter XI

As Elijah Brown deposited his bicycle in his rooms and dressed for dinner, he wracked his brain for conversation topics. He feared that if he mentioned all the cancellations his patients had made that day, Kitty would think ill of his medical competence —or at least of his business acumen. On the other hand, he was quite sure nobody wanted to hear about Silas Hayes' bowel movements, especially over dinner.

He kept trying to come up with ideas as he walked to Kitty's rooms, but when he got there his brain felt as empty as an overturned pail.

The rooms Kitty shared with Miss Bray had their own entrance at the back of their landlady's house. As Elijah approached through the garden he saw that the outer door was already open, likely in an attempt to lure a cool breeze into the rooms.

He stopped to compose himself, and it suddenly occurred to him that he should have brought flowers. He frowned and the action brought his gaze downwards towards the forget-me-nots lining the walkway. The significance of the fact that he was standing in a garden suddenly dawned on him.

He looked up at the windows of the house, then checked over his shoulder. Seeing no one watching, he quickly plucked some bachelor's buttons, love-in-a-mist and marigolds from behind a rose bush where he thought they wouldn't be missed. He tried putting them in some semblance of an artistic arrangement, but finally decided that such a thing was beyond any man's capabilities.

When he'd dressed for dinner earlier he'd switched his watch back from its short cycling tether to its usual chain. On his walk over here, and just now picking the flowers, the chain had slipped so that it hung lower over one side of his waistcoat than the other. He evened out the chain, straightened his waistcoat, and took a deep breath before walking the final steps to Kitty's door.

The smell of frying salmon wafted out deliciously. Through the open door, Elijah saw Kitty leaning over a small parlor stove, tending a skillet on top of it. Her cheeks had a lovely, rosy flush from the heat, and the light streaming in through an open window shaded her figure to breathtaking effect. She looked so beautiful standing there, Elijah found his carefully gathered composure leaving him again.

The oil from the fish was making loud sizzling sounds, and Elijah had walked up so cautiously he wasn't surprised that Kitty hadn't heard him. He tried to clear his throat or swallow, but his tongue seemed to have turned to blotting paper.

Kitty knelt down in front of the stove, and a pretty frown creased her brow as though she were dissatisfied with the apparatus. Elijah thought her petulant expression only made her look more charming.

She shrugged to herself, stood up again, and shut the stove's damper to douse the fire. She lifted the skillet, and as she turned towards a waiting platter with lemon wedges and fresh dill all around its edges, she saw Elijah watching her.

"Oh!" She started back. The skillet shook in her surprised hand but she didn't drop it. "Dr. Brown! I— I'm sorry, I didn't see you there." A deeper red crept into her cheeks. "Come in, come in! Just—" Her eyes darted down at the fish, then up at him again. "Could you please just give me a second?"

She transferred the fish to the platter, then disappeared behind a folding Japanese screen. When she reappeared again, the skillet was gone.

"Thank you for coming!" She gave the man a smile so warm it melted him.

"Thank you for having me." He held up the flowers in a sweaty hand. "I hope you like these."

"They're lovely!" Kitty responded automatically at first, then gave the blossoms a quizzical look. "You know, my landlady grows flowers just like—"

"I hadn't noticed!" As soon as he blurted the words, Elijah realized he'd spoken too quickly for credibility.

Kitty gave him a slightly surprised look, then a knowing smile. "They're lovely," she repeated. "Absolutely lovely."

She went into her bedroom and returned with the flowers in a vase from her wash-stand, filled with water from her ewer. In a few deft motions she transformed the clump of flowers into the artful arrangement Elijah had attempted but given up as hopeless. Then she put them on the table and shut the outer door. As she moved around the room he couldn't tell which was louder: the rustle of Kitty's silk petticoats, or the beating of his own heart.

"How was your day?" She asked.

It was the last question he wanted to answer. He said something non-committal about it being uninteresting, then stopped. "I mean—" he corrected, mentally kicking himself. "Nothing interesting happened *except* for your visit, of course!"

A smile pulled up the corners of Kitty's mouth as she served salad and salmon onto two plates. Then she suddenly stopped, and looked at the table with an expression of dismay as though she'd forgotten something. She opened her mouth, then closed it again. She looked pointedly towards the window. "Don't you think my landlady has a lovely garden? Miss Bray and I always enjoy it."

Brown took the hint, and walked over to the window. The light was just right for the glass to act as a sort of mirror, and he turned his back on Kitty he watched her actions by observing her reflection. As soon as he seemed distracted by the garden, she hurried over to a table in a corner of the sitting room. On it sat something large, poofy, and covered with lace. Elijah had assumed it was a pillow of some kind, although he hadn't understood why it was sitting on a table. Kitty lifted up the lace and he heard a hinge creak. When he turned around again there was a loaf of bread on the table next to the salmon platter. He almost made a joke about loaves and fishes, but held his tongue.

Between the hidden bread and the trick with the skillet behind the screen, Elijah realized he was seeing clues to the mysteries that perplex every bachelor: why single women's apartments always seemed so artistically cluttered, and how they managed housekeeping without visible traces of any of the things that made it possible. He wondered what else Kitty might be able to teach him about women.

He swallowed hard and tried to think of something to say. "I'm glad your headache's better," he told her. After a pause, he asked, "How did the rest of your day go?"

A pained expression came over Kitty's face, then she sighed heavily. "Oh, not very interesting," she told him, clearly borrowing from his description of his own day. "I don't suppose you know anyone who might want a dress made out of sixteen yards of peacock green silk, do you?"

The question surprised Elijah, but at the same time it reminded him of the scene over Silas Hayes' fence. David Goldstein had said his wife would fill in as Hayes' housekeeper until a new one came, and that she'd want to spend her wages on a new dress. A fancy new silk dress.

"Well," Elijah told Kitty thoughtfully. "Actually, I might."

Kitty's eyes lit up, in a way that made Elijah want to keep that light there, always. "Really?" She asked. "Who?"

He explained the situation with the Goldsteins and Mr. Hayes.

Kitty sighed slightly, and it seemed to Elijah that it was a sigh of relief. "That would help," she told him. "Would you mind asking her if she'd be interested?"

"I'd be happy to," he answered sincerely.

"Here—" She went over to her bookshelf and pulled out the April edition of *The London and Paris Ladies' Magazine.* "Show her this." She turned to the third fashion plate, then took a mechanical pencil off her chatelaine and circled the figure in the middle. She handed the magazine to Elijah. "Nothing sells a dress faster than a picture of it finished." She smiled at him, and he almost thought he'd be willing to pay for the dress himself if it could keep that sweet expression on Kitty's face.

When they finished their supper Kitty looked thoughtfully at the leftover fish. "You know," she commented, "I've got another piece of salmon in my refrigerator that's just as big as the one we started with. Would you like to take this one home with you, maybe have it for lunch tomorrow?" She looked sideways at Dr. Brown and one corner of her mouth turned upwards in a sly grin. "It would save you from Mrs. Ostergren's cooking for another meal!"

Elijah laughed. "That sounds like a good plan!"

She turned the remaining fish and bread into a sandwich, wrapped it in brown paper and tied it with string.

When she handed it to him their fingertips brushed together. Neither could have said whether it happened by accident or design, but to each the touch was like light in a dark room.

Kitty was struck by how strong Elijah's hands were, yet how soft his fingertips. *Of course they would be,* she reflected. *He's a doctor.*

Elijah felt the sewing calluses on Kitty's fingertips and thought of how hardworking her hands were, yet at the same time how fine and delicate.

Kitty stood up on tiptoe and pressed her lips against Elijah's. Then she looked into his eyes and smiled. When roses crept into her cheeks she shyly turned away, but he gently cupped her chin in his hand. She rubbed her cheek against his soft fingertips. He tenderly tilted her face to meet his again.

Outside the window, two brilliantly colored woodpeckers were building a nest in Kitty's garden.

Chapter XII

Early the next morning, the bright light of a nearly full moon streamed through Elijah's window and woke him from a dream about Kitty. As he climbed from bed, it seemed as though the vibrant sensations of the dream were still with him: the soft feel of Kitty's golden hair, the taste of her rosebud lips. The sound of her silks.

As he put on his cycling outfit he thought of her making it. He ran his fingers along a seam and pictured Kitty's hands there. He swallowed hard.

The Ostergrens weren't awake yet as Brown slipped quietly out of the house with his bicycle. He rode out to a hill past the edge of town and leaned his wheel against a tree. The sandwich and magazine Kitty had given him were wrapped in a towel and strapped them onto his handlebars along with his medical roll; he took the sandwich out and sat down on the cool, pungent earth, facing the sunrise. As he untied the string and unfolded the brown paper, he thought of the different ways Kitty had been taking care of him lately.

He watched the rosy dawn creep over the trees and thought of what it would be like to wake up every morning to Kitty herself, instead of just a dream of her. He remembered how peaceful she had looked when he'd seen her asleep, and imagined watching the morning light spill over her golden hair.

He ate speculatively, and after he'd finished he tossed the paper into the woods. He told himself that if he ever wanted to have money to marry he'd best get to work. Then he set out on his rounds.

The bicycle gave him a chance to visit patients he hadn't seen for months.   First he rode twenty-five miles to check on a hermit fur-trapper, then he visited a family on a remote farm in Beaver Valley and vaccinated their twins. The older children at the farm were fascinated by Dr. Brown's bicycle. At their request he circled the farmhouse to show how the machine worked. They tried running after him but couldn't keep up, yet they gleefully called for him to put on still more speed. It was a refreshing change from the last couple days.

On the way back to Chetzemoka he stopped at a logging camp, and found himself just in time to treat a man whose foot had been crushed when one of the big draft horses stepped on it. He took care of the situation and got back on his bicycle. As he rode back to town he reflected that (despite yesterday's cancelled appointments) he might still have a viable practice after all.

It was late afternoon when he got back to Chetzemoka. The Goldsteins lived a short distance within the city limits and Brown had brought Kitty's fashion magazine with him so that he could make a quick stop there on his way back downtown and fulfill his promise.

The Goldsteins' kitchen door and window looked out onto the road. As Brown rode up on his bicycle he heard a low, appreciative whistle.

"Now *that* is a beautiful machine!" Mr. Goldstein was home from work already; he leaned out the window with an admiring expression on his face.

Brown made a smooth dismount right in front of the door and smiled at him. "You like it? I guess you didn't see it yesterday."

"No, Doc. I'd remember a machine like that!" Goldstein's grin stretched from ear to ear.

Dr. Brown laughed. "Mr. Goldstein, I don't think I've seen you this excited about something since the sawmill got a new boiler!"

Goldstein nodded his head, then gestured to someone behind him. "Rachel! Rachel, come see this!" He went out through the kitchen door, Mrs. Goldstein right behind him.

Goldstein peered at the center of the wheel. "Are those ball bearings?"

"Yes!" Brown answered proudly.

Mrs. Goldstein politely pretended to look interested as the men discussed this detail.

Goldstein fingered the knurled adjuster. "Ingenious! What a machine —look at all the nickel-plate!"

Mrs. Goldstein pulled some chickweed out from around the chives growing under her kitchen window and tossed it in an empty flowerpot.

"Are those bearing pedals as well?"

Brown looked a little embarrassed. "No," he admitted reluctantly. "Those are just the standard bushing pedals."

Mrs. Goldstein scraped some dirt out from underneath her fingernails. When the men continued their conversation she started discretely moving back towards the kitchen.

Dr. Brown saw her trying to get away and remembered the reason he had dropped by. He called after her, "Oh, Mrs. Goldstein!"

Rachel Goldstein froze. The look on her face reminded Brown of a girl who'd just been caught trying to sneak away before her mother could remind her it was her turn to scrub the floor. "Yes, Dr. Brown?"

He loosened the straps on his handlebars and slid the magazine from under his medical roll. "I heard you're interested in a new silk dress."

Rachel perked up immediately as Dr. Brown opened the magazine and turned to the third fashion plate. "I happen to know that Mrs. Butler has all the materials for this one in stock—" He pointed at the one Kitty had circled. "—If you're interested."

Mrs. Goldstein devoured the plate with her eyes. "Now, *that* is a dress! Look at that sash! And the gilet and train!"

Mr. Goldstein went back to examining the bicycle's cranks.

With a smile, Brown handed the magazine to Mrs. Goldstein. "Would you like me to tell Mrs. Butler a time you'll drop by to be measured for—?"

His question was interrupted by the sudden, shrill sound of a steam whistle, coming from the sawmill.

Dr. Brown and Mr. Goldstein both looked towards the mill in surprise, then simultaneously took out their watches. As they read the time, both men's faces took on the same grave look.

The doctor grabbed his bicycle and shot off towards the mill.

Rachel Goldstein looked towards her husband, concern in her kind brown eyes. "It's not quitting time at the sawmill yet, is it?"

"I'm afraid not." He solemnly put his watch away.

Her eyes followed the swiftly disappearing doctor. "Was that—"

David Goldstein nodded grimly. "The emergency signal," he affirmed. "There's been an accident at the mill."

Chapter XIII

The Goldsteins' place was only a few miles from the mill, and Brown's wheel ate up the distance rapidly. When he got there, all the workers were out front crowded around a young man. His face was ashen, but he was standing unaided. In a voice made unnaturally high by strain, he was telling the crowd, "He saved me! It would have been my head that log bashed in if he hadn't shoved me out of the way! And now—"

Brown dismounted, unstrapped his medical roll in a swift motion and let his bicycle drop.

"Where's the hurt man?" He demanded, pushing through the crowd.

A chorus of deep voices told him. "The office!"

"Get the foreman there, too!" Dr. Brown ordered, setting off for the office at a run.

Behind him, he heard the men call, "Doc, the foreman's already there! Bill Clapper's the one who's hurt!"

The office door was shut, but Brown let himself in without knocking. A man's voice (not Clapper's) yelled, "I told all of you to stay—"

As he came in the room Dr. Brown's eyes met those of the mill owner. He was kneeling down by a prostrate Bill Clapper, and his tone changed abruptly when he saw the doctor. "Dr. Brown! Thank God you could get here so fast!" He stood up and moved out of the doctor's way. "He's in pretty bad shape."

The curtains on the room's windows were closed, probably to keep the workers from staring in. Bill lay on a large board supported between two strong crates. Someone had already removed his shirt and it was laying in a shredded heap on the floor. His left shoulder was clearly out of its socket, and there were unnatural angles in that arm. His chest had a disturbingly concave look on the left side where several ribs were obviously broken. He was grimly still.

"Give me light!" Dr. Brown ordered, kneeling by his patient. "What happened?"

The mill owner re-opened the curtains, bringing light into the room. "One of the ropes broke when the men were lifting a log. The new kid was right in its swing path, leaning over. The log would have bashed his skull in if Clapper hadn't jumped in front of it to push the kid out of the way. The log got Clapper instead."

Bill's eyes were closed. His breath was shallow, but he was breathing.

"Bill, you awake?" Dr. Brown asked loudly, checking for other signs of consciousness. "Bill, can you hear me?"

Bill muttered something. The only words Brown could make out were "fool kid".

"I'm gonna get you fixed up, Bill," Dr. Brown promised.

He went to work.

Chapter XIV

Bill Clapper had three broken ribs, but luckily none had punctured a lung or any other organ. Dr. Brown wrapped Bill's chest and got the dislocated shoulder back in place. He was setting Bill's broken arm when one of the other town doctors arrived.

When the man expressed astonishment that Brown could have arrived so quickly, the bicycling doctor smiled privately and concentrated on his patient.

"Hey, new Doc," Bill spoke up woozily, raising his head towards the newly arrived physician. "You got any more of that morphine?"

Brown shook his head at the other doctor and gave Bill a wry look. "I've already given you enough to knock over a horse. Just bide there, now."

Bill grumbled and lay his head back down.

Dr. Brown put splints on Bill's arm, then checked him all over again to make sure he hadn't missed anything and that the patient was as comfortable as possible. He gave him a few instructions, then asked Bill where he lived so he could check on him the next day.

As Brown re-rolled his medical kit, he caught the other doctor's eye and nodded towards Bill. "Never hurts to have a second opinion," Brown commented. He went outside, leaving the other doctor with Bill to double-check his work.

Most of the mill employees had dispersed. The owner remained outside, and a handful of men were clustered around the young man who had narrowly escaped a fatal injury from the log which broke Bill's ribs and arm.

Brown had a talk with the owner about Bill's condition and how long the foreman would have to recover before getting back to work. The doctor noticed the workers glancing at them repeatedly throughout the conversation. When they finished talking they beckoned him over.

"Mr. Clapper gonna be alright?" One of the men asked.

"Should be," Dr. Brown responded. "He'll have to take things easy for a while, but I expect he'll be back here bossing you men around again before too long."

The men looked —well, not relieved, exactly, but approving. They might not like Bill Clapper, but they clearly respected him.

The one individual who did look unambiguously happy at the news was the young man Bill had saved. He was a young pup about nineteen years old, and introduced himself as Ivan Johnson.

"Hey, Doc—" He caught Brown just as the doctor was turning to leave. "Anybody could tell you Clapper's not gonna show any gratitude for what you did, but I'm thankful for it. Why don't you come over to my family's house for supper tonight? My ma's a great cook. My sister's getting married in a few months and it's her beau's birthday so he'll be there with a bunch of his friends and their wives and sweethearts." Ivan smiled broadly.

Faced with the happy prospect of avoiding his landlady's cooking for the second night in a row, Brown gladly accepted the invitation.

The other mill men called the kid aside and whispered something to him. A few of them cast smirking glances at Dr. Brown, but they looked mischievous rather than malicious. The kid grinned and told the doctor, "Bring that pretty young widow Butler to the party with you!"

Chapter XV

Elijah dropped by Kitty's rooms to tell her about their invitation and hastily left her to get changed while he sped home to do the same. He put on a regular suit for the night and left his wheel in his room, then headed back out again to meet Kitty.

The address Ivan had given Dr. Brown was on the far end of Chetzemoka, and the road leading out to it started halfway between Elijah's rooms and Kitty's. He waited for her at the crossroads, and when he saw her coming she nearly took his breath away.

She was in a beautifully fitted black dress with red trim and white lace all down the front. He bowed and offered her his arm. She blushed as she took it.

"I owe you a big thanks," Kitty confided as they walked down the road. "Mrs. Goldstein came by this afternoon —she's such a nice lady. She put in an order for that dress we talked about."

Elijah smiled and nodded. "I'm sure she's looking forward to it."

Kitty laughed. "My land, yes! It's been a while since I've seen someone quite that excited about a new dress. I'm surprised she hasn't been in to see me before, liking clothes that way."

Elijah rubbed his chin. "I think last time the Goldsteins had a windfall money-wise they were still paying off their move out here. As I recall, they came here because the trade unions back east were making it hard for Mr. Goldstein to get work. They've only been in Chetzemoka a few years."

The story touched Kitty's tender nature and a sadness crept into her eyes, but then she smiled and said with conviction, "Well, the East's loss is the West's gain! From what she was telling me, her husband has plenty of work now. If this is her first nice dress in a while, I'll take extra care with it. Thank you for sending her to me."

"I'm glad I could help."

They walked in silence for a while, enjoying each others' company in the warm, flower-scented evening.

As they walked up to the house Kitty realized she had no idea who their hosts for the evening were. She turned to face Elijah and asked, "Now, whose birthday did you say it was?"

"Well, it's—" He stopped and laughed at himself. "Actually, I'm not really sure. His future brother-in-law invited us. Nice young man named Ivan Johnson."

Kitty looked startled. "Johnson? Elijah, this isn't—?"

The door opened and Ivan ushered them inside before Kitty could finish her question or Elijah could ask why she suddenly seemed so distressed.

"So glad you could come, Doctor Brown, Mrs. Butler! When I got back home from the mill things were already so busy with all Mr. Dunn's friends showing up I couldn't get a word in edgewise. I never got a chance to tell my family I'd invited you. But don't worry, Ma made plenty!"

Kitty tried to interrupt, but Ivan kept right on talking, in a slightly lower voice. "I'm sorry, my ma insisted on inviting Reverend Curlew. I tried at least to seat you as far as I could from the old sourpuss. You're sittin' right by my sister."

The stricken look on Kitty's face intensified by several degrees. If Elijah hadn't been a doctor he might have thought she had suddenly become ill. Behind Ivan's back he mouthed, "What's wrong?"

Kitty just shook her head and followed Ivan with the expression of a brave martyr entering a lion's den. Elijah gave her his arm. When she leaned on him gratefully he squeezed her hand and gave her his most reassuring expression.

Ivan showed them to the last two vacant seats at the table, next to a couple who were cooing over each other. He started to introduce them as his sister and her fiancé, but when Miss Johnson looked up and saw Kitty an expression of intense mortification overcame her face.

The fiancé (Ezra Dunn, according to Ivan's introduction) was seated at the wrong angle to see his betrothed's expression when she faced the newcomers. In marked contrast to his sweetheart's face, Mr. Dunn offered Kitty and Elijah a broad, welcoming smile. "Doctor Brown!" He pumped Elijah's hand vigorously. "I'm so honored you came to my birthday party! And Mrs. Butler, such a delight to see you! Last week Flora was telling me how excited she is about the bridal gown you're making for her. I've been out of town since last Thursday so I haven't heard any of the latest details. Do tell me how it's going."

Kitty stood speechless, looking at Flora Johnson with a pale face and pressed lips.

Miss Johnson was in a short-sleeved party gown, and from the play of muscles within her arms Elijah could tell that under the table she was wringing either a handkerchief or a napkin into nervous contortions.

The two women faced off wordlessly. Mr. Dunn, Elijah and Ivan exchanged increasingly confused glances. At last Kitty suggested, "I'm afraid you'll have to ask Miss Johnson why she cancelled her dress order."

"What?" Mr. Dunn looked shocked. "Flora—"

Just then, Mr. Johnson came in with the roast, suspending all conversation.

Reverend Curlew said an interminably long grace. As soon as he finished, Flora Johnson stuffed her mouth unbecomingly full of bread so that she would have an excuse not to talk. One of Mr. Dunn's friends proposed a toast for many happy returns of the day, then one was proposed for the health of the happy couple.

Kitty picked at her food without appetite. Elijah squeezed her hand under the table, and she smiled at him.

Mr. Dunn whispered a question to Miss Johnson, presumably about the cancelled wedding dress. She gave a low response and he started back in surprise. He glanced down the table at

Mrs. Johnson, then over at Kitty and Elijah, then back at his fiancée again.

"Come on, you love birds!" One of the young women at the table teased. "No whispering at supper! Let us in on your secret!"

"Or if you're just cooing things that would turn our stomachs," a man said with a snicker, "tell us *a* secret, at least!" There was a bump under the table, as though someone had kicked the speaker.

Mr. Dunn looked down thoughtfully and pulled on the shorter side of his watch chain to make it hang evenly with the other half. "Actually, it seems Flora and I have just encountered our first difference of opinion. It concerns whether or not something is bad luck."

A soft groan went around the table.

From the movement of the table cloth on his lap, Elijah could tell that Kitty's fingers were locking and unlocking nervously under the table. He took her closer hand in his again and held it tight. He had no idea why such a strange argument between the lovers should so agitate Kitty, but through the tender grasp of his hand he tried to communicate that he was there for her.

"Reverend Curlew—" Mr. Dunn continued. "Would you be so kind as to give us an educated churchman's opinion on superstition?"

Reverend Curlew was seated at the far end of the table next to Flora's mother. It took a sharp eye to notice that when young Mr. Dunn asked the minister about superstition, he was looking at Mrs. Johnson.

Mr. Dunn's friends stifled yawns and occupied themselves with their suppers. Any one of them could have detailed what Curlew's answer was going to be, yet Flora Johnson looked very unlike someone about to lose an argument. She seemed more like a woman who was about to finally get her own way after a long debate. Like her fiancé, her eyes were on her mother instead of the minister.

"Why certainly, my boy!" Curlew began expansively. "Superstition is a relic of heathen barbarism. To say that something is bad luck or good luck has no place in a Christian society..."

As Curlew continued to drone on, Kitty held her head higher and stared straight at Mrs. Johnson, who looked increasingly uncomfortable.

Finally Mrs. Johnson leaped up from the table and said she'd better start washing dishes. Flora Johnson slipped away on the pretense of helping her mother.

Mr. Dunn put an end to Curlew's sermonizing by proposing a toast to enlightenment, and a visible sigh of relief went around the table.

Someone asked how Elijah and Kitty happened to be invited that evening and Ivan launched into an excited account of the incidents at the mill. The senior Mr. Johnson congratulated Elijah on his quick presence at the emergency, and said he wished doctors could have gotten more quickly to some of the logging camps where he'd worked.

"Actually, I was just at a logging camp earlier today," Elijah responded, and told the story of the logger with the crushed foot.

At the conclusion of the story Mr. Johnson smiled and raised his glass approvingly. "Well done, Doctor Brown!"

A chorus of "Here, here!" went around the table, and Kitty raised her own glass. "To the wheel 'As true as truest horse that yet would never tire'!"

A laugh went up from the more educated among the company assembled, and everyone drank.

Reverend Curlew looked down thoughtfully, then around at the assembled company. "Well, it's true that there are wheels within wheels!"

This time everyone laughed.

Flora Johnson came back into the room with a victorious smile on her face, and resumed her place next to Mr. Dunn. She turned towards Kitty and opened her mouth, then looked suddenly contrite. It took her a moment to start again. "Mrs. Butler, Ma said I could put that order for the wedding dress back in with you." She looked down embarrassedly. "That is, if you'll let me."

Kitty gave Flora Johnson a long, searching look. "Well, I did just get in an elaborate order for a carriage dress. It'll keep me busy for a while."

Flora's face fell, and tears gathered in the corners of her eyes. "Mrs. Butler, I— Please? I'm so sorry for what I said yesterday."

Kitty nodded, satisfied. "I'll do it."

Some of the men around the table asked Elijah to tell them more about bicycles, and he related the story of seeing them for the first time in Boston. The women at the table seemed particularly interested in the idea of all those cyclists showing off their shapely calves.

"But, is there no equivalent machine for women?" A young lady asked.

Kitty perked up her ears. She'd never thought to ask that question.

Elijah grinned. "Yes—tricycles! Rumor is that even the queen of England has a couple of them!" When a few people around the table frowned, trying to picture the machine in question, Elijah explained: "A tricycle has three wheels instead of two. The rider sits between the wheels instead of on top." He grinned, and stretched out his legs under the table. "Besides women, some old men ride them, too."

The conversation continued late into the night, and several men asked very pointed questions that made it clear they were interested in bicycles themselves. Eventually the party broke up as people recalled that they had work in the morning.

There were so many questions about bicycles, Elijah and Kitty were some of the very last to depart. When they finally took cordial leave of their hosts, Flora Johnson insisted they borrow her lantern. She promised she would come by Kitty's dress shop the next day to go over some details of her re-instated order, and said Kitty could give back the lantern then.

118

It was such a beautifully clear night they really only needed the lantern when passing under trees. On clearer sections of road where logging had already been accomplished, the sky above them was flooded with a sea of gleaming diamonds.

Elijah insisted on walking Kitty all the way to her rooms, even though this left him to walk home without a lantern. He said he didn't need one on such a night. Before handing it over though, he used its light to find a particular flower he had seen in Kitty's garden the day before. He plucked a long stalk of bright pink blooms and handed it to her. "Do you know what this one's called?" He asked, a twinkle in his eye.

She smiled with all her heart and tilted her chin upwards. "Kiss me over the garden gate!"

He did.

Chapter XVI

The next spring was a particularly beautiful one in Chetzemoka. The woods around town were filled with vibrant pink rhododendrons. Young women with keen eyes could spot wild orchids in the underbrush: ladyslippers, coralroot, ladies' tresses and Venus slippers. In the gardens of uptown grew more civilized flowers: tidy daffodils and stately irises, respectable marigolds and unrestrained love-in-a-mist. Lilies of the valley emerged, sweetly-scented, from moist places and announced their message in the language of flowers, "Return to happiness." Everywhere, in woods, farms and town, camas lilies sprouted in unexpected places where squirrels and chipmunks had stashed bulbs they'd stolen from Indian fields.

There were a few more bicycles in town now. Sewing riding clothes for the cyclists had been a pleasant sideline of Kitty's dress business over the winter, although none meant quite as much to her as the first pair she'd created.

Men who couldn't afford a wheel of their own yet were saving for one, and subscriptions to cycling magazines were a regular sight passing through the Chetzemoka post office.

On a glorious morning when the sky seemed quilted over with cerise silk, the rising sun showed the church on the hill to be overflowing with flowers placed there late the night before. There was to be a wedding that morning.

A few blocks away in the rooms Miss Bray was soon to have all to herself, Mrs. Goldstein was helping the bride with her hair.

"It's such a pretty, pearl-gray silk you chose for your dress, Kitty," Mrs. Goldstein commented, pinning a wild orchid in Kitty's hair. "Did you know we'd find Venus slippers when you chose the taffeta for your trousseau's petticoats? They match so well."

"I hoped we would." Kitty lifted her gown's skirts until blushing pink silk was revealed.

"It'll make a nice flash of color when you move," Mrs. Goldstein observed. "It's a pity the wedding's indoors. On such a lovely day..."

Kitty laughed. "That's the third time this morning you've said we should have had an outdoor wedding!"

"It just seems so much more natural." Mrs. Goldstein shrugged.

Kitty laughed again. "Be satisfied that the dinner is out of doors." She glanced towards the window with her eyes, trying to keep her head still for hairdressing purposes. "I wonder what the bicyclists have been conspiring about? Elijah won't tell me a word of it, but I know those men are up to something."

Mrs. Goldstein shrugged. "David's been sneaking off to watch them practice something, but he hasn't told me what."

"Hmm..."

Mrs. Goldstein pinned a final orchid in Kitty's hair and stepped back to admire her handiwork. "I think you're nearly ready."

"Almost." Kitty took a pretty bouquet from a vase on her dresser. She dabbed gently at the dripping stems with a hand towel, and tied them with a wide, blue satin ribbon.

"Those lilies of the valley smell heavenly," Mrs. Goldstein commented. "I noticed them as soon as I walked in the room. The yarrow and balm of gilead set them off nicely, too."

Kitty smiled softly, gazing down at the flowers. "I thought they were all appropriate."

"Quite right," agreed Mrs. Goldstein. She noticed a slight moisture in Kitty's eyes, and gave her a handkerchief. "There, now."

Mrs. Goldstein gave Kitty a moment, then held out her hand and gently helped her up. "Ready?"

Kitty took a deep breath, bit her lip, then smiled. "I think so."

"Then I'll have my husband tell the groom's party," Mrs. Goldstein said, and went out.

After she left, Kitty looked in the mirror and thought back on another day, when her dress had been white and the flowers in her hair were orange blossoms.

There was a framed cabinet card on Kitty's dresser; she lifted it and gazed at the man in the picture. He didn't look much like Elijah, but Kitty remembered how he'd had the same contagious enthusiasm for life that drew her to him. She smiled, and kissed the picture. "I think you would have liked each other," she told the man in the photo, and set it back down.

There was still a sprig of forget-me-nots in the flower vase; Kitty moved them over and arranged them in front of the photo, then smiled again. She walked out of her rooms and through the garden, along a path lined with lilies of the valley.

Chapter XVII

Everyone agreed it was a beautiful wedding, and even Reverend Curlew was seen indulging in a few smiles when he seemed to think no one would notice.

A few men who witnessed the wedding were suspiciously absent from the crowd offering congratulations afterwards, but if anyone noticed, no word was mentioned. The newlyweds had eyes only for each other, and everyone else's attention was consumed by the beauty of the day.

The supper was laid out on a table outside the church. When the wedding party and guests started gravitating towards the feast, a small child called out that there was a bird on the table.

All eyes followed the child's tiny, pointing finger, and saw a brightly colored flicker stealing fresh currants off a tray. People moved to shoo it away, but Kitty called to them to leave it alone. Elijah concurred, and wrapped his arms around his bride.

"It's only right," he whispered in Kitty's ear. "After all, he shared his wedding with us."

The newlyweds kissed, and the assembled crowd applauded. The flicker took wing, carrying away a bunch of bright red currants with him.

When the sound of applause died away, a small chorus of tinkling bells could be heard approaching. It soon grew louder, and five bicyclists appeared riding braced against each other with arms linked. As they came closer, the

crowd heard hearty singing by masculine voices.
Those who recognized the tune joined in:

"Sweet love of mine,
My soul and thine
Are linked by hidden chains,
My life with thine will intertwine,
While life itself remains.
The roses rare that scent the air,
In winter fade away,
But joy or care with thee I'll share,
My heart, my heart is thine alway...
But joy or care with thee I'll share,
My heart, my heart is thine alway...

Sweet love of mine, my soul did pine
In loneliness unblest,
This love of thine on me did shine,
And brought me peace and rest.
The swallow flies to kinder skies,
When early fades the day,
My summer lies within thine eyes,
My heart, my heart is thine alway...
My summer lies within thine eyes,
My heart, my heart is thine alway..."

Apendix:

This story has been the first in a series of novellas about the adventures and romances of a cycling club in the Pacific Northwest in the late nineteenth-century. Thank you for purchasing it! I hope it has brought you as much enjoyment to read as it brought me to write, and that you will be sure to tell your friends about it! Be sure to read the next installment, *Love Will Find A Wheel.* For inside details about the series, visit http://www.thisvictorianlife.com/tales-of-chetzemoka.html

The town of Chetzemoka is fictitious, but it owes a lot to the real city of Port Townsend in Washington state —my home. Founded in 1851, Port Townsend experienced a boom in the 1880s. A great deal of beautiful architecture still survives here and draws people to a town which prides itself on being a Victorian seaport. In the late nineteenth-century there was an actual dressmaker named Pussy Butler with a shop in downtown Port Townsend; and the schoolteacher's name was Lizzie Bray, just like in the novella. Their names are all I borrowed though: the characters in this story are entirely fictitious.

The name Chetzemoka is an homage to the chief of the Clallam tribe. Many American cities are named after local tribes or their leaders: Seattle (named after a Duwamish chief) is a great example.

I created the fictitious city of Chetzemoka (rather than setting the tale in historic Port Townsend) to give myself leeway to make a few changes for dramatic purposes. The biggest of these was bringing the sawmill town of Port Gamble closer to the action. Port Gamble (founded in 1853) is a little over twenty-seven miles from Port Townsend —about fifty-five miles roundtrip. I've biked there and back myself, but in the story it would have been an unrealistic distance for a horse to race at full gallop. (Attempts at long distance bicycle vs. single horse races in the 1880s often killed the horse, though the cyclists came out just fine.) I took a fiction writer's liberty of relocating things to suit my story's needs, and made the sawmill an adjunct to the town. Visitors to modern Port Townsend will see a paper mill (built in the 1920s) in the precise location where I placed Chetzemoka's sawmill. Other changes were more minor: for example, I gave Kitty Butler a dress shop in the Hastings Building in 1881, although the real Hastings Building in Port Townsend wasn't built until 1889. Similarly, the fire bell tower was built in 1890. But, these are the liberties one takes in fiction.

In everything substantive about the culture and technology of the time, I made every effort for scrupulous accuracy. I hope the following notes and links will help you with your own research and inspire you to seek out even more information about the era:

—For more about everyday life in the Victorian era, be sure to check out my website: www.ThisVictorianLife.com

—The idea of a boarding-house cook using fish skins to clear coffee (and ruining the coffee in the process) comes from the article "Six Cups of Coffee Prepared for the Public Palate", by Mrs. Helen Campbell, *Good Housekeeping*, June 11, 1887. p. 61.

A digital version of the magazine is available here: http://tinyurl.com/jrjmxdh

—The phrase "I vum" was lower-class slang in America in the 1800's; it comes from the phrase "I vow" and essentially means "I'd swear to it" or "I'm sure".

—The comment about a bicyclist excelling "the fleetest horse" on "any course longer than five miles" is taken from "A Wheel Around the Hub." *Scribner's Monthly*, February, 1880, p. 481.

—Reverend Curlew's sermon on the importance of observing the sabbath is a direct quotation from "On Sunday Riding," a letter written by John St. George in 1883 and quoted in *Outing and The Wheelman*, October, 1883, pp. 65-66. His speech about wearing one's best apparel at church comes from the book of sermons, *Social Dynamite*, by T. DeWitt Talmage, Chicago: Standard Publishing Company, 1888. p.348.

—The carriage dress order Kitty created for Mrs. Goldstein is from Figure 2 (#91) on Plate 3, *The London and Paris Ladies' Magazine*, April, 1881, description on p. 3. A digital version of the magazine is available here: http://tinyurl.com/gq8m5p7

—Dr. Brown's musings on how useful a bicycle is to a physician are borrowed from an article by a real, historical Victorian physician: "Physicians and the Bicycle" by George S. Hull, M.D. *Outing and The Wheelman*, October, 1883, pp. 57-58.

—An article on the use of quinine in epilepsy (like the one Dr. Brown was reading) appeared in *The Ohio Medical Journal,* August, 1881, p. 79. An article on milk indigestion appeared in the same magazine, November, 1881, p. 232.

—U.S. President James A. Garfield was shot on July 2, 1881 but didn't die until September 19th of that year —hence, the medical journal Brown is reading in late August is discussing the president's treatment after the "attempted" assassination.

—The vaccinations Dr. Brown gives the twins at the farm would have been for protection against smallpox. In the late nineteenth-century all Americans were very emphatically urged to have themselves and their families vaccinated, and in England the procedure was required by law.

For information about the history of vaccines, see http://www.historyofvaccines.org

—The scene of Kitty buying salmon from Indians selling baskets on the beach was inspired by an 1895 photograph. It is currently in the University of Washington's archive and can be viewed here: http://tinyurl.com/z4u73c3

—The descriptions of the Kitty's lodgings owe a lot to two different *Good Housekeeping* articles: "An Old Maid's Paradise", March 30, 1889 and "A Word Fitly Spoken", August 3, 1889.

—In the nineteenth-century, "refrigerator" was the most common term for the appliance now more usually called an ice box. For more on this, see the article "Ice Boxes vs. Refrigerators" by Jonathan Rees: http://histsociety.blogspot.com/2013/12/iceboxes-vs-refrigerators.html For a description of living with a Victorian refrigerator, see http://www.thisvictorianlife.com/kitchen-and-dining-room.html

—Kitty's toast, "As true as truest horse that yet would never tire" is from *Midsummer Night's Dream*, iii, I, and was suggested as a toast for a bicycle meet in *Quotations for Occasions*, The Century Co, 1896, p. 177.

—The song "Sweet Love of Mine", with words by S.M. Samuel and music by Fred Cowen, was published in *Peterson's Magazine*, March, 1881. Sheet music for the piece can be found here: http://tinyurl.com/z2d8o93

—For more on Port Townsend, WA, see: www.porttownsend.weebly.com

—For daily posts about the Victorian era giving quotes from the period and fun facts about the time, be sure to like my author page on Facebook: https://www.facebook.com/ThisVictorianLife/

It's been a pleasure to share this story with you. Best of luck on all your projects!
—S.C.

Further Tales of Chetzemoka!

Love Will Find A Wheel
By Sarah A. Chrisman

"I'm sure he'll be glad you're here —once he gets used to it."

When Jacob Simmons arrives in Washington Territory in the summer of 1882 and receives a glacial reception from his uncle Silas, he appreciates Dr. Brown's encouraging prediction but doesn't have much faith in it. Jacob's not even sure Silas will have time to get used to his presence, let alone consider him welcome. If the young man can't meet the draconian requirements of a contract with his business investors, he'll face exile and financial ruin, thus fulfilling old Silas' prediction that he would be just as dismal a failure as his father. His whole future rests on finding a market for a remarkable new machine —and he'll need help selling them.

***

Addie Kellam is an incredibly lonely young woman. She's more comfortable with books than with other people, yet she longs for the sort of romance she reads about in stories. It's something she fears she'll never experience herself, since even friendship seems elusive. She envies the cameraderie her brother finds in his cycling club, but the only bicycles in the town of Chetzemoka are specifically designed for men. There aren't any wheels for women anywhere —are there?

Made in the USA
San Bernardino, CA
29 September 2016